P9-CCE-653

3 1192 01445 4845

Death Trap

"Out of the way!" I yelled, even though I doubted Frank could hear. I made a move toward the entrance path.

But it was already too late. The edge of the plow clipped the wooden wall of the operator's shed, its sharp, spinning blades digging chunks out of it and sending them flying like deadly missiles. I spun toward the other end, but the plow was scraping against the rock wall on that side, sending out a shower of sparks.

We were trapped!

SEP 2 3 2009

THE HARDY BOYS

Undercover Brothers®

Available from Simon & Schuster

HARDY BOYS

Undercover Brothers

BOYS

FRANKLIN W. DIXON

#30 The X-Factor
Book Three in the Galaxy X Trilogy

EVANSTON PUBLIC LIBRARY
CHILDREN'S DEPARTMENT
1703 ORRINGTON AVENUE
EVANSTON, ILLINOIS 60201

Aladdin
New York   London   Toronto   Sydney

If you purchased this book without a cover, you should be aware that this book is stolen property. It was reported as "unsold and destroyed" to the publisher, and neither the author nor the publisher has received any payment for this "stripped book."

This book is a work of fiction. Any references to historical events, real people, or real locales are used fictitiously. Other names, characters, places, and incidents are the product of the author's imagination, and any resemblance to actual events or locales or persons, living or dead, is entirely coincidental.

ALADDIN
An imprint of Simon & Schuster Children's Publishing Division
1230 Avenue of the Americas, New York, NY 10020
First Aladdin paperback edition September 2009
Copyright © 2009 by Simon & Schuster, Inc.
All rights reserved, including the right of reproduction
in whole or in part in any form.
THE HARDY BOYS MYSTERY STORIES is a trademark of
Simon & Schuster, Inc.
ALADDIN PAPERBACKS, HARDY BOYS UNDERCOVER
BROTHERS, and related logos are registered trademarks
of Simon & Schuster, Inc.
For information about special discounts for bulk purchases,
please contact Simon & Schuster Special Sales at 1-866-506-1949
or business@simonandschuster.com.
The Simon & Schuster Speakers Bureau can bring authors
to your live event. For more information or to book an event contact
the Simon & Schuster Speakers Bureau at 1-866-248-3049
or visit our website at www.simonspeakers.com.
Designed by Sammy Yuen Jr.
The text of this book was set in Aldine 401 BT.
Manufactured in the United States of America
10 9 8 7 6 5 4 3 2 1
Library of Congress Control Number 2009922706
ISBN 978-1-4169-7802-2
ISBN 978-1-4169-9655-2 (eBook)

TABLE OF CONTENTS

FRANK

1

Bombs Away

"Aaaah!" I yelled as my mountain bike's front tire skidded on a patch of mud. At the speed I was going over the rough wooded trail, a wipeout would be a disaster.

I wrenched the handlebars to one side, slipping through the mud at a forty-five-degree angle to the ground. Somehow the bike kept going and I managed to get it upright again. Whew!

The bike I was chasing was only a dozen yards ahead now, its rider crouched over the handlebars. Just then the ground dropped away in a steep downhill incline. There were big, jagged rocks embedded everywhere in the packed dirt. I had to pay attention so I wouldn't hit any of them with

1

my front tire and wind up flying head over heels over the front of the bike.

"Left! Left!" my brother Joe shouted from somewhere behind me.

Glancing up, I saw that he was right. Our quarry was veering off to the left, taking a narrow uphill trail through some tall pine trees.

I leaned over the handlebars and pumped the pedals as hard as I could. Seconds later I skidded around the corner at breakneck speed. By then the other bike was already slowing down. The hill was massive.

Even in the heat of the chase, I couldn't help being impressed. This had to be the best mountain biking trail I'd ever seen. And the most amazing part? It wasn't in the wilds of the Rocky Mountains or anywhere like that. No, it was part of Galaxy X—a brand-new amusement park on an island off the Carolina coast. I guess with enough money, you could build anything. At least that seemed to be the philosophy of Tyrone McKenzie, the super-successful music producer who'd created the place.

"Stop!" I yelled as I pumped up the hill. "Come on, Lenni. We just want to talk to you!"

The biker glanced back briefly. I was ready to put on more speed. This wasn't the first time

Lenni Wolff had led me and Joe on a wild chase. Lenni was a local skateboarding phenom. She had moves that even professional skaters couldn't top. She also had a major attitude about Galaxy X. That was partly because McKenzie had razed the old skate park she and her friends had built on the same site. It was also because she disapproved of the very existence of a place like GX. Anyone willing to pay the entrance fee could come in and try out a bunch of extreme sports along with the roller coasters and other regular theme park rides. Lenni thought that cheapened real skater culture.

She wasn't the only one who felt that way. There was all kinds of buzz about it on the Internet. Even a website called StopGX. Besides that, local protesters had been picketing outside the place since before it opened.

That was how Joe and I had ended up there. McKenzie had called in ATAC to figure out who was behind some online threats and real-life vandalism. ATAC stands for American Teens Against Crime. It's a super-secret crime-fighting organization started by our dad after he retired from the NYPD. It sends in agents like Joe and me to investigate in locations where adult agents might seem out of place. Locations like GX.

The biker ahead slowed even more after I

called out. I put on a last burst of speed, my leg muscles screaming. But it was worth it—I caught up. Grabbing Lenni by the shoulder, I yanked her off the bike.

"Hey!" The other biker hit the ground hard, then sat up and glared at me from under his helmet.

Hang on. *His* helmet?

Oops. "Um, sorry, dude," I stammered out, backing away. "Thought you were someone else."

Just then Joe skidded to a stop nearby. "Where's Lenni?" he panted, glancing around. "And who's that guy?"

I sighed. "Come on, bro. Let's take the bikes back in. It looks like Lenni outfoxed us again."

A few minutes later Joe and I were heading out of the mountain-biking attraction's equipment shack. We reached the main path and stopped.

"What now?" Joe squinted against the bright midday sun and glanced up and down the path. "Should we keep looking for Lenni?"

I shook my head. "Not much point. If she wants to keep out of sight, she will."

"Why's she still playing keep-away?" Joe sounded perplexed. "After that stunt she pulled with Cody Zane's skateboard, she's, like, a hero!

McKenzie probably wants to give her a medal or something."

"Or something." I grimaced as I noticed a paper flyer lying on the ground nearby. I didn't have to pick it up to guess what it was. Lenni and her crew had been passing out anti-GX screeds ever since the place opened. "He thinks she tried to blow up Cody Zane just now, remember?"

That was what had set Joe and me on this chase. An hour or so earlier, world-famous skateboarder Cody Zane had started a demonstration. But he'd lost his balance and come off his board on a basic move. Weird, right?

But Joe and I had quickly figured out what was up. Someone had attached a bomb to the bottom of the board. Its weight had thrown off Cody's balance. Only Lenni's quick thinking and even quicker reflexes had saved the day. She'd hopped on the board and quickly built up speed on the half-pipe. Then she'd flown upward, kicking the board up into the air. It had exploded harmlessly up there, saving Cody and everyone nearby from being blown to bits. In all the commotion afterward, Lenni had disappeared into the crowd.

And now Joe and I wanted to find her. But *not* because we agreed with McKenzie's opinion that she or her friends must have planted that bomb.

No way. For one thing, Lenni was the one who'd risked her life to get rid of the bomb. Besides that, she just didn't seem like the type. She was way passionate about her beliefs—she'd even been arrested in the past for protesting and stuff. But ATAC's best researchers hadn't turned up anything in her past to show she'd be willing to hurt people in pursuit of her goals.

Still, we wanted to talk to her. Lenni was pretty tied into the local and online skate communities. We figured if anyone could help us work out who was still trying to sabotage GX, it was her. For instance, we hadn't yet tracked down the real identity of an online agitator who went by the name Sk8rH8r. Or figured out who'd planted that bomb on Cody's skateboard.

Speaking of Cody . . . I started to reach for my cell phone. Then I remembered. Lenni had stolen it from me earlier. She'd said she wanted a way to keep in touch.

"Rats," I muttered. "Hey, Joe, can I borrow your phone? I want to call Mr. McKenzie and find out what's up with Cody."

Joe smirked. He's always been the scatterbrained one in the family. It would take both hands and feet to count the number of times he's lost or broken his expensive ATAC-issue cell phone. He was pretty psyched that I'd been the one to mess up this time. Like it was my fault Lenni had opted to pick my pocket instead of his!

"Sure, Frank," he said, pulling out his phone. "But please, allow me to make that call. I wouldn't want you to accidentally lose my phone too."

Yeah. He's a laugh riot.

A few minutes later we had the update. Cody was still at the local hospital. It sounded like he was going to be okay, but he did have a pretty decent concussion. They were flying him to a bigger city hospital within the hour.

"Sounds like he probably won't be back." Joe frowned as he tucked his phone back in his shorts pocket.

I was tempted to pay back his earlier razzing by teasing him about his fanboy attitude toward Cody. Even though we'd discovered that Cody was kind of a jerk, I could tell Joe was still impressed by him. So I kept quiet about that.

"So what do you think?" I asked instead. "Could David have rigged up that skateboard bomb before he got arrested?"

David Sanders was our latest perp in the case. Yeah, I said latest. First we'd discovered that one of the protesters and his nephew, a GX security guard, had been behind some of the vandalism.

But when the trouble continued—and got even worse—we'd kept investigating. Eventually we figured out that Cody Zane's friend and skating partner, David Sanders, had been targeting Cody to get back at him for selling out and neglecting their friendship.

Joe shrugged. "It's possible David did it," he said as we wandered past GX's state-of-the-art arcade. "But according to McKenzie, he's still denying it. Besides, it's not like that's the only loose end on this case."

"True. So maybe we should go over things." I glanced up at the skeletal remains of the park's huge man-made mountain. Mount McKenzie—yeah, the guy named it after himself—had been the centerpiece of Galaxy X. It had stood five hundred feet tall at the intersection of the two main paths through the park.

But not anymore. Someone had blown it up during the park's grand opening. Now it was pretty much a big smoking pile of rubble covered with a bunch of blue tarps. And none of our perps would admit to demolishing it.

"Well, there's *that*, of course." Joe waved a hand toward the mountain. "Along with all the online threats and mysterious e-mails and stuff."

"Right," I agreed. "Neither of our culprits have fessed up to being Skater Hater. David was For-Real, but he says he has no idea about Skater Hater."

"And Lenni won't cop to it either. Not sure I believe her on that."

"I believe her, actually," I said. "Whoever Skater Hater is, he had our e-mail addy, remember? And he started sending us stuff before we'd ever even met Lenni. Plus, he seems to know whenever something bad happens around here."

"Yeah, and so does Lenni. She's always popping up when there's trouble," Joe argued, though his heart didn't seem to be in it. "Okay, but what else is there? Oh yeah—you and Cody almost getting sliced and diced by that messed-up roller coaster."

I shuddered at the memory. It had happened on a coaster called the Leap. Its gimmick was that the cars jumped over a break in the track and landed on the other side. Only someone had messed with the landing side of the track so that our car had ended up plunging over the edge and crashing into the metal support structure. If Cody and I hadn't managed to jump out in time, it would've been our last ride. Luckily, the thing wasn't officially open to the public yet, so nobody else had been at risk.

"Anything else?" I asked. "Oh wait, I remember—there was that rock that someone threw at Erica outside the gates."

Erica was Tyrone McKenzie's eighteen-year-old stepdaughter. She'd been with Joe and me when we'd gone outside the park gates to check out some people who were protesting GX's opening.

"We probably shouldn't get too caught up in that one. It could've been that crazy old coot Jackson, even if he wouldn't admit it. Or it could've even been one of the other protesters."

"I guess you're—," I began.

KA-BOOOOOOOM!

An ear-shattering explosion from somewhere nearby cut me off before I could finish.

2

A Total Blast

"It's the bomber!" I shouted, already running in the direction of the explosion. "He's struck again—come on!"

Frank was right on my heels. We sprinted down the path and around the corner by a snack stand, following the noise and smoke.

When I reached the source, I screeched to a stop. Standing there in front of one of the rides was Tyrone McKenzie. He was smiling. That was kind of a change. He wasn't exactly Mr. Cheerful at the best of times. And lately? Well, you couldn't really blame him for being in a bad mood. Though it was kind of hard to feel sympathetic sometimes when he was screaming at us.

His whole family was with him. They were all smiling too. Okay, some of the smiles looked kind of forced. But they were smiling.

"Hold it!" a woman's voice called out. There was a click and the whirr of a camera shutter.

McKenzie's gorgeous young wife, Delfina, giggled loudly. "Wait, can we do another take?" she trilled. "The little prince grabbed my hair right when you shot that one. I think the noise startled him, poor thing."

She shook her long blond hair out of her face and hoisted Tyrone Jr. to her other hip. The baby let out a cheerful squeal and grabbed for his mother's hair again. McKenzie shot the pair a slightly impatient glance. Erica just sighed, while McKenzie's son Nick rolled his eyes and scowled. Yeah. One big happy family . . .

"What's going on here?" I murmured to Frank, eyeing the gray smoke still swirling around the scene. A massive man with a gleaming bald head was fiddling with some equipment nearby. That equipment seemed to be the source of the smoke—and presumably the noise we'd heard.

"Looks like some kind of photo op," Frank whispered back.

"Ready, Mrs. McKenzie? Okay, hold it, everyone. Just a couple more frames . . ."

I glanced over at the photographer who'd spoken. She was fiddling with the lens of her camera while another couple of photographers snapped away. There was a video camera, too, which was capturing the whole scene. Okay, so I got the publicity thing. McKenzie loved that stuff. But why had they set off that blast?

Then I turned to check out the ride behind the McKenzie family. It was one I hadn't really noticed before.

"'Bomber Pilot,'" I read off the sign over the little wooden control hut beside the ride. Okay, now I got it. "Sounds cool."

Frank frowned. "I thought this ride wasn't going to be ready to open for a couple of weeks. Nick said something about it when we had dinner with the McKenzies the other night."

Leave it to Frank. He remembers every little detail, even the boring ones. Okay, *especially* the boring ones. Me? I'm more of a big-picture man. I guess that's why we make such an awesome team.

"Really? Are you sure he was talking about this ride? Because it sure looks like it's about to open," I pointed out.

"I'm positive. Don't you remember? Nick kept muttering and complaining about how he wanted to try it out—kind of acting like his dad had delayed it on purpose just to spite him."

That sounded like Nick. He and his dad didn't exactly get along. Maybe he resented the fact that McKenzie had dumped Nick's mother and remarried—twice. First to Erica's mom, then to Delfina, who was only a few years older than Nick himself.

Not that he could complain too much, in my opinion. Delfina's picture was probably in the dictionary under the word "hot."

To distract myself from that thought, I took a better look at Bomber Pilot. It was a type of swing ride—a bunch of cars dangled from a central pillar. The cars were shaped like mini fighter planes, each of them attached to the pillar by two massive chains.

"Hmm," I said. "Doesn't really seem up to GX's standards, does it? I mean, it's just another swing ride."

"Not quite," Frank corrected. "For one thing, the center part oscillates so the swing-out is unpredictable. Besides that, there's laser technology that lets riders try to shoot at holograms of enemy planes while they're riding." Off my surprised look, he added, "Read about it during my research on this place."

I rolled my eyes. Frank's middle name might as well be "Research." But I had to admit the ride did sound pretty cool. Plus, it fit right in with the patriotic military theme of this section of the park. I glanced up at the nearest roller coaster, known as Old Glory, and then over at the entrance to some kind of military tank attraction we hadn't had a chance to check out yet.

By now the photographers were packing up their equipment. McKenzie looked up and saw us.

"You two!" he barked out, hurrying over. "Find that Wolff girl yet?"

I'd just started wandering toward the neighboring attraction, curious for a better look at the full-size tanks parked in there. But now I hurried back. Not that it made much difference. McKenzie never paid much attention to me when Frank was around. He claimed Frank reminded him of himself at that age. Whatever. I was just happy to be out of the line of fire most of the time.

"Not yet, sir," Frank was replying. "Er, is Bomber Pilot opening soon? I thought it wasn't ready yet."

McKenzie scowled and glanced over his shoulder at the ride. "Well, we *made* it ready," he snapped. "I mean, I had to do *something* to replace all those attractions that got wrecked in the explosion. Not to mention take everyone's minds off the disaster that this grand opening has been!"

He had a point. When Mount McKenzie had exploded, the park's guests had thought it was just part of the show. But there were tons of reporters and other media types around for the grand opening, and they'd figured out the truth soon enough—especially since the demise of the mountain meant that most of the attractions located on its slopes were kaput too. That meant no more downhill skiing, no rock-climbing walls, no snowboarding—you get the picture.

McKenzie had managed to pass it all off as an accident with the opening-day fireworks. But when more stuff kept going wrong, it got harder to explain away. Stuff like Frank and Cody almost getting filleted by the Leap. Or various other attractions breaking down. And especially the death of superstar boy bander Bret Johnston, who'd been electrocuted by a microphone David Sanders had rigged for Cody. Yeah, that one was going to be tough to keep quiet. Based on what Frank and I were hearing around the park and seeing online, people were starting to think GX was cursed.

I noticed that McKenzie had turned to glare at Baldie over at the smoke machine or bomb simulator or whatever it was. I looked that way too. The dude was huge. Muscle on top of muscle. I'd seen him around the place ever since we'd arrived—he was hard to miss!—but I wasn't sure who he was.

"Okay, thanks for the info, sir. I was just curious," Frank was saying in his superpolite Eagle Scout way. "I was under the impression that there was a lot more work to do on this ride, that's all."

"There was," McKenzie snapped sourly. "My people are working triple-time to get it ready to open tomorrow. It was the only one we even had a shot of finishing in time. I mean, things are all messed up over at the Jungle, so that was out. And the morons who were supposed to deliver the safety barriers and whatnot for Whitewater Wipeout just called to say they're delayed *again,* and the stupid inspectors won't let us open the ride without them."

He degenerated into a round of cursing. Then he turned and stabbed a finger toward Baldie. "Make sure the crew gets back on the job right away!" he yelled. "If this ride isn't ready to go first thing tomorrow, heads will roll!" With that, he stomped away. I glanced at Baldie. If looks could kill, McKenzie would be in about the same shape as the mountain he'd named after himself. Yikes. Whoever he was, Baldie was one scary-looking dude.

"Guess we're all finished here!" Delfina trilled. She hoisted Tyrone Jr. onto one shoulder and toddled away on her four-inch heels.

The photographers were all gone by now too. Nick and Erica drifted toward us. I wasn't thrilled to see Nick—the guy was kind of a dweeb. But Erica was another story. Not only was she easy on the eyes, but she was smart, too. Our first day there, she'd hotwired one of the roller coasters to take us for a ride. I mean, what's hotter than a cute girl gearhead?

"You guys are still here?" Nick said. Then he smirked. "Oh, right. You still haven't figured out who's trying to wreck this place. Bummer for you. In case you couldn't tell, my father doesn't like losers."

I gritted my teeth as he hurried off. Meanwhile Erica sidled up to Frank, standing so close they were almost touching. I hid a grin as Frank's face went beet red. Okay, it was pretty annoying that she had the hots for him. I mean, what was I—chopped liver? Still, watching my nerdy brother's reaction to her obvious crush made for some top-flight entertainment.

"So what's up with the case, anyway?" Erica tilted her head up at Frank. "I assume it's open again?"

"Looks that way," the lobster that had taken over

my brother's body replied. "David Sanders claims he had nothing to do with that bomb on the skateboard. Plus, we still haven't figured out who blew up Mount McKenzie—Sanders wasn't even here yet when that happened."

I nodded. "Looks like there might be someone else around here who doesn't like GX. Or your stepfather." I looked at Baldie again. He'd gone back to fiddling with the equipment.

"But don't worry," Frank was telling Erica. "We're on the case. We'll do our best to track down the culprit before anyone else gets hurt."

Erica touched Frank on the arm. "I love it when you talk like that," she cooed. "You know—all the secret agent stuff."

Frank opened his mouth to answer, but nothing came out. Instead his face just got redder than ever.

I could hardly hold back my laughter this time. Frank could be so lame that sometimes it was hard to believe we were related.

Still, I decided it might be time to come to his rescue. If he spontaneously combusted, I'd be stuck finishing the mission on my own.

"Yeah, the first thing we need to do is talk to Lenni Wolff," I told Erica.

She looked surprised. "That skater chick? You really think she's behind all this?"

"Nope," I replied. "But we're hoping she can help us figure out who might be."

Erica nodded. Then she checked her watch and grimaced. "Oops, I've got to go," she said. "I'm stuck with babysitting duty today."

"Bummer," I said.

She rolled her eyes. "Yeah. Especially since Delfina takes, like, all day whenever she goes to the hairdresser over on the mainland. Guess it takes time to create that shade of blond that's not found in nature."

She said good-bye and hurried off. "So I guess this means we're back on Lenni patrol?" asked Frank. His face was already returning to its normal color.

I shrugged. "Might as well, unless you've got a better plan." We headed toward the main path. "By the way, who's Mr. Clean back there?" I added.

Frank glanced back over his shoulder. "You mean Ox?"

"Okay, Mr. Clean, Ox, Paul Bunyan, whatever you want to call him."

Frank chuckled. "No, that's his name," he said. "Ox Oliver. He's the head of maintenance for the whole park. Don't you pay attention to anyone who's not a cute girl?"

"Hey, we can't all be lady-killers like you,

Mr. Smooth," I shot back. "Just ask your girl-friend Erica."

That shut him up for a while. We kept walking. Finding Lenni in the crowds seemed like a hopeless cause. But we were also keeping an eye out for anything suspicious. Until we figured out who was behind the latest mischief, it was impossible to guess when or how the culprit might strike again.

About an hour later, we ran into Nick. He was leaning on the fence, watching a bunch of guests enjoy the demolition derby attraction. When he spotted us, he hurried over.

"Yo, I just heard your good pal Lenni Wolff is causing trouble again," he said with a frown.

"Really? Where?" I asked.

"Cliff diving."

"Thanks for the info. Come on, Joe." Frank was already breaking into a jog.

The cliff-diving attraction was way off in one corner of the park. Actually, the "cliff" was built out from the high perimeter walls over there. It looked pretty realistic. Divers plunged down into one end of an enormous man-made lake that also held a bunch of boating attractions.

When we got there, we found a chain stretched across the entrance. A sign on it read SORRY, WE'RE CLOSED.

"Why's it closed?" asked Frank. "Wasn't McKenzie just talking about how important it is to keep stuff open?"

"Maybe our friend Lenni has something to do with it," I said, ducking under the chain. "Let's go see what she's up to."

A narrow set of steps led directly up to the cliff wall. The top was hidden from us most of the way up, though anyone walking along the shores of the lake had a great view of people diving. It would be a fantastic choice for someone who wanted to attract a lot of attention—like Lenni.

"Maybe she's up there trying to hang one of her anti-GX banners," I panted as we took the steps two or three at a time.

But when we reached the top, there was no sign of Lenni—or anyone else. The place was deserted. The door of the operator's shed was ajar, and a huge tractor with an even huger plow attached was parked a few yards back from the edge.

"So where's Lenni?" I stepped carefully around the enormous, sharp-looking plow blades to peer over the edge of the cliff. No banner. "And what's with the farm equipment? Are they planning to plant corn up here or something?"

"Maybe that's how McKenzie's planning to make back all the money he's losing from the sabotage," Frank quipped, joining me at the edge.

I looked down at the gleaming expanse of water below. "Wow, this is cool!" I said. "How'd we miss this place before? I hope they open it up again soon so we can give it a try."

From the look on Frank's face, I could tell he was about to remind me for the millionth time that we were at GX to work, not play. But before he could open his mouth, we heard an ominous rumble behind us.

"What's that?" Frank turned to look. His eyes widened, and he let out a shout.

But I could barely hear it. That's because the tractor's engine had just started up with a roar. It immediately lurched forward.

"Out of the way!" I yelled, even though I doubted Frank could hear. I made a move toward the entrance path.

But it was already too late. The edge of the plow clipped the wooden wall of the operator's shed, its sharp, spinning blades digging chunks out of it and sending them flying like deadly missiles. I spun toward the other end, but the plow was scraping against the rock wall on that side, sending out a shower of sparks.

We were trapped!

High Dive

"Come on!" I yelled directly into Joe's ear. I hoped he could hear me over the roar of the engine. "There's only one way out—straight down!"

We rushed back to the edge of the cliff. A few seconds ago diving off it had looked like fun. Now, not so much. I took a deep breath. . . .

"Yeaaaaaaaaaaaargh!" I shouted as I leaped off the edge.

Nearby, I could hear Joe yelling too. Most of my attention was on the sparkling sheet of water approaching extremely rapidly below. Out of the corner of my eye, however, I caught a glimpse of the enormous tractor tipping over the edge of the cliff and falling after us. Whoa. Suddenly the dive itself didn't seem like the scariest part of this. Not by a long shot.

SPLASH! I hit the lake at an awkward angle. But I recovered quickly, kicking and pulling at the water for all I was worth, hoping I was going in the right direction. If not, I was going to be in a world of hurt when that tractor splashed down. . . .

A few seconds later there was an enormous *WHOOOOOOOOSH!* as the tractor hit the water. The wave that went up swamped me, sending me back underwater and tumbling head over heels. But the tractor itself missed me by at least a few feet. Whew!

My head was spinning and I wasn't sure which way was up. I just aimed for the light, hoping my air held out. When my head popped up again, I gulped in gratefully. For a second I thought my ears were still ringing from the noise of the tractor. But no. It was actually the distant sound of cheering. That was weird. But I had other things on my mind.

"Joe!" I shouted hoarsely. "Where are you?"

My brother's head popped up at that moment. He was only a few feet away. I was surprised we hadn't bumped into each other underwater. I smiled with relief.

Then I finally looked over at the shore. A bunch of people were gathered there, staring our way. Some were cheering. Others were jumping up and down, pumping their fists.

"Guess they thought that was part of the GX show," I said breathlessly.

Joe spit out some water. "Yeah," he said. "McKenzie can call it Tractor Diving. It'll be a huge hit. Come on, let's go in and let someone know what happened."

A few minutes later we were onshore, wringing the water out of our clothes. "Yo, that was awesome, dudes!" Some random park guest shouted, hurrying over to us. "This place is killer!"

Yeah. He could say that again.

Most of the spectators seemed to agree with the first guy. But a few were looking nervous.

"I dunno," one skinny little teenager mumbled. "I heard this place might be, you know, unsafe. Like, for real."

Joe and I traded a surprised look. "Hang on," Joe said, grabbing the guy as he started to wander off. "What are you talking about? Who said it was unsafe?"

The dude shrugged. "Read it on a website," he said. "You know—that StopGX one. Said there were a bunch of accidents. People getting hurt. Stuff like that."

"Whoa," Joe murmured as the guy took off. "I thought our man Tyrone was keeping a pretty good handle on publicity. Guess not, huh?"

"Even McKenzie can't control the Internet. Especially if someone here is feeding inside info to the webmaster." I bit my lip. "Are you thinking what I'm thinking?"

"Only if you're thinking Lenni could be that someone." Joe shot a glance out toward the lake. It was pretty deep in the spot where we'd landed, and the surface had closed over the tractor, giving no hint that it lay beneath. "But she wouldn't have done *that*, would she?"

"You mean try to kill us?" I shook my head. "Doubtful. Actually, I still don't think she's behind any of the dangerous stuff. But I definitely wouldn't put it past her to spread bad publicity about this place. That's kind of what she's all about."

"Good point. So then who just tried to take us out?"

I was wondering the same thing. "Do you think the tractor thing was meant for us specifically?" I mused, rubbing my chin and staring up at the cliff. "Or was it just more sabotage against the park in general?"

Joe's eyes widened. "I don't know," he said. "But come to think of it, someone sure sent us over here—you know, specifically."

"Nick," I said, realizing he was right. "You think he had something to do with it?" McKenzie's son had been a suspect for a while earlier. We'd speculated that he might be sabotaging the park as a cry for attention from his distant father. He hadn't turned out to be the culprit that time. But that didn't necessarily let him off the hook for the new stuff.

"Dunno," Joe said. "But it's worth asking him a few questions, don't you think?"

I nodded. "Let's call McKenzie and tell him what happened. Then we can look for Nick."

Joe fished his cell phone out of his shorts pocket, shook off the water, and flipped it open. Luckily, it was working despite the dunking. McKenzie didn't answer, so Joe left a message on his voice mail. Then we set out to find Nick, also keeping an eye out for Lenni.

We were still looking for both of them half an hour later when we noticed a hubbub near the main gate. "What's going on over there?" I wondered aloud.

"One way to find out." Joe took off at a jog.

I followed. There were tons of people milling

around in the main plaza. We pushed our way through until we could see the area right in front of the gate. There, about a dozen people—mostly teenage and preteen girls—were standing around holding up posters, T-shirts, and CDs. Most of them were sobbing or wailing.

"Hey," Joe said. "Looks like some kind of teeny-bopper vigil for the late Mr. Bret Johnston."

I nodded. "Guess McKenzie couldn't really keep that news from getting out."

It had been less than two days since Johnston was killed. If this many distraught fans were here already, I could only imagine how many more were on their way. And I had a feeling McKenzie wasn't going to be happy about it.

"Bret! Bret!" the girls wailed at the top of their lungs. Then several of them started singing an out-of-tune version of one of Bret's band's biggest hits, "(No More) Mr. Nice Guyz." Soon all of the mourners were singing along.

The vigil was really drawing a crowd. Even the protesters from outside were peering in curiously through the gates.

"Come on." I turned away, deciding we might as well take advantage of the uproar if we could. "Maybe it'll be easier to scout around the park while everyone's distracted here."

"Sounds like a plan," Joe agreed.

We'd barely gone two steps when the sounds of angry shouting came from nearby. Glancing over, I saw several security guards dragging a young woman toward the gate.

"Let me go!" she was screeching, clawing at the guards. Her long, straight brown hair was falling over her face, which was streaked with tears. She looked pretty hysterical. "You have to let me go! This is an outrage!"

"That's enough, miss," one of the guards said firmly. "We're going to have to ask you to leave now, before we get the police involved."

"You can't stop me, and neither can the cops!" the young woman shrieked wildly, breaking loose from the guards and almost crashing into some of the younger Bret fans. "I'll never leave the site where my beloved Bret died. Never! And if you try to make me, you'll be sorry. You'll *all* be sorry!"

Fanning Out

"Okay, call me crazy, but that kind of sounded like a threat," Frank said as the guards caught the nutty Bret fan and dragged her outside.

"You're crazy," I said automatically. But I was already drifting after the guards. That skateboard bomb had turned up after Bret died. Not to mention us almost getting plowed under by that tractor. Could this crazed fan be trying to avenge her idol's death or something? It seemed pretty whacked-out. Then again, criminals aren't always rational.

The guards finished ejecting the young woman, though we could still hear her yelling outside. Most of the guards hurried back inside, but one stayed in the entry, keeping an eye on the woman. Guess he drew the short straw.

Frank and I hurried over to one of the others. "Hey, what was that all about?" I asked.

The guard glanced at me. He was a big, beefy guy with a gold tooth. For a second I thought he was going to brush us off.

But then one of the other guards joined him. "Yo, aren't you the two secret agents?" the second guy asked us.

I winced. McKenzie had totally blown our cover by telling the media he'd brought in a pair of secret agents to figure out who was sabotaging the park. Obviously, the guests at the park still had no idea who we were. But it hadn't taken long for most of the staff and crew to figure it out.

"So what did she do?" I asked, not really answering the question.

The first guard rolled his eyes. "She came this morning with the rest of 'em, I guess." He gestured toward the younger fans, who had resumed their crying and singing. "All I know is we got a call that she was trying to pry up the floorboards off the stage."

"Huh?" Frank looked confused. "What do you mean? Why would she do that?"

The second guard grimaced. "Said she wanted

to keep the ones that Johnston guy was standing on when he died. Pretty sick, huh?"

"That's not all." A third guard had overheard our conversation and wandered over. "Ox says she's been causing trouble all day. She already stole bits off a bunch of other attractions—all the places where Bret Johnston shot publicity photos, pretty much. Even managed to pry loose one of the rocks at the edge of the cliff-diving wall."

Well, that explained why the cliff-diving attraction was closed. I figured that Ox dude must have ordered it shut down until it could be checked for safety. But where did the giant tractor come in?

Before I could figure that one out, Frank elbowed me in the side. "Come on," he said as the guards wandered off. "Let's see if we can talk to her."

"You think there's something here?"

"Who knows? But you heard what they said about the cliff-dive thing. What if she was the one who left that tractor up there? She might've driven it up to help her snag that rock, then left the parking brake off or something."

"Sounds kind of far-fetched," I said doubtfully.

"Yeah. But we're not exactly rolling in better theories right now, at least until we track down Nick or Lenni."

He had a point. We hurried out through the gates. The regular bunch of GX protesters was gathered out there. All of them were sort of hanging back, keeping a wary eye on Miss Superfan. I couldn't blame them. She looked pretty crazed.

"Excuse me, miss?" Frank was already hurrying over to her. "Can we ask you a few questions?"

She glared at him suspiciously. I couldn't help noticing she was actually kind of cute. "What do you want?" she snapped.

When she lifted her arm to brush back her hair, I saw that she had a large tattoo of Bret Johnston on her wrist. Whoa. Now that was hard-core fandom.

"What's your name?" I asked.

"Zana Johnston. What's it to you?"

"Johnston?" Frank echoed. "Wait, you're not actually related to Bret Johnston, are you?"

"Only in spirit." Zana's eyes fluttered half-shut, and she let out a melancholy sigh. "I knew from the first time I saw him on TV that Bret and I were soul mates. That's why I legally changed my last name to match his. I was sure that one day we would meet, and he would realize our destiny too." She ran the fingers of her other hand over her tattoo. "But now it seems we were never destined to meet in this world."

"Um, okay." Frank is pretty good at keeping his cool in even the weirdest situations. But this was pretty weird even for him—he was starting to look a little wigged out.

"So we heard you were up on the cliff-diving wall," I put in. "Did you, um, drive a tractor up there?"

"What?" Zana looked confused. "Why would I do that? Wait, did Bret drive a tractor while he was here? I didn't hear anything about that! You have to tell me everything!"

I had the feeling that if we said that Bret's magical backside had ever so much as touched the seat of that tractor, she'd rush back in and drag it out of the lake with her bare hands. It was tempting to try it and see. But I knew Frank wouldn't approve of that.

"No, sorry for the confusion," said Frank. "Er, thanks for talking to—"

"I still can't believe my Bret is gone!" Zana clutched at her hair. Actually, it looked like she might have pulled out a handful. "It just doesn't seem real. . . ."

She went on like that for a while. Frank and I stood there and listened. I don't know about him, but I was just waiting for a good moment to bolt.

Then I noticed Lenni heading our way from the parking lot. She didn't seem to notice us at first.

Instead she headed straight for the group of pro-testers. They were still hanging back from crazy Zana.

Lenni walked up to one of them, a frizzy-haired woman who looked about forty. Frank and I had talked to her a few times, so we knew she was a local resident who was concerned about the environmental impact GX would have on the islands. Lenni seemed to know her too. She handed the woman a PowerUp sports drink and chatted with her for a moment.

Then she finally spotted us and hurried over.

"Hey," she said to us as Zana paused for breath. "I heard you guys were looking for me."

Zana blinked at her. "Who are you?" she demanded. "Are you here to help memorialize Bret too?"

Lenni looked confused. "Who? Oh, you mean that singer who croaked the other night?"

Zana looked outraged. "Don't you dare speak that way of my Bret!" she cried. "It's bad enough that fate has wrested him from this life without having to listen to such things!"

"Fate?" Lenni's mouth twisted into a wry little smile. "Well, you might want to check with the cops, but I'm thinking fate didn't have much to do with it."

"What?" Zana yelped. She looked so freaked out that I expected her head to start spinning around. "What are you talking about? Are you saying Bret's death was the result of foul play?"

It was all I could do to keep from rolling my eyes. I mean, who talks like that? Frank and I are in the business, and even we hardly ever use phrases like "foul play."

Zana clenched her fists and shook them at the heavens. "I swear, if I find out someone is responsible for my love's early demise, I'll make them pay! Mark my words!"

Then she rushed for the gate and started arguing with the guard. I felt sorry for the guy.

"Is she for real?" Lenni said, staring after her.

Frank shrugged. "I guess she's pretty upset about Bret Johnston's death."

"Yeah, I get that." Lenni shook her head. "I mean, I saw those teenyboppers earlier, okay? But really, what kind of grown woman gets so freaked over some lame celebrity? Seems almost too crazy to be true, you know?"

"What do you mean?" I asked. "You think she's faking?"

"Maybe." Lenni lifted one shoulder. "She could be a plant. You know—someone Tyrone hired to act nutty enough to make all the protesters and vigil holders look so bad that the cops will come and clear them out once and for all."

I exchanged a dubious look with Frank. "Whatever," I said. "But listen, we really do need to talk to you. . . ."

We moved out of earshot of the rest of the people outside the gates. Then we told Lenni about the cliff-diving incident. She seemed surprised to hear it.

"Cliff diving?" she said. "I thought all that kind of stuff blew up with the mountain."

"Not this," Frank said. "It wasn't part of Mount McKenzie. It's over in the northwest corner by the boating lake."

"Oh. Well, I don't know anything about it."

"Okay," I said. "But you should know McKenzie thinks you had something to do with that skateboard bomb."

She frowned. "Are you for real? I saved his stupid park by kicking that bomb up in the air! If it'd gone off and taken out Cody Zane, GX would've been history for sure. Even Tyrone McKenzie doesn't have enough dough to bribe his way out of *two* celebrity deaths!"

"You have a point," said Frank. "And I'm not saying *we* think you did, okay? But obviously someone did it, and we need to know who. Along with who blew up Mount McKenzie. And who messed with the Leap the other day and almost got me and Cody killed."

Lenni scowled at him, kicking at a rock on the pavement. "Believe me or not, I don't care. But I'm telling you, it wasn't me. I don't know anything about who messed with that board, or the explosion, or the rumors on StopGX, or any of the other stuff."

Hang on. We hadn't even mentioned StopGX. . . .

Before I could say that, my cell phone rang. It was McKenzie.

"I want you two over here right now," he barked when I answered. "There's been an incident at the RCA park!"

5

Fight or Flight

McKenzie hung up before Joe could say a word. "So what's an RCA park?" Joe asked after he told us what McKenzie had said.

"That's easy," Lenni spoke up. "RCA stands for radio-controlled aircraft." She smirked. "In other words, it's where overgrown little boys can go play with their remote control toy planes."

"Oh, right." Now I remembered seeing the place. "Come on, we'd better get over there and find out what's up."

We said good-bye to Lenni and headed back inside the gates. "So what kind of trouble could there be with model planes?" Joe asked as we jogged down the main path.

"Guess we'll find out."

When we reached the RCA park, McKenzie was practically sputtering with rage. A small group of celebrities clustered nearby. A bunch of model aircraft lay scattered lifelessly on the grass. They actually looked pretty cool. There was everything from a miniature World War II Luftwaffe fighter to a model of the Wright Brothers' plane.

"I thought most of the celebs left after the preview thing," I murmured to Joe. "After Bret Johnston died and Cody got hurt, none of them seemed too eager to stick around, even with all the VIP treatment."

Joe shook his head. "Some of them are still hanging out. I saw Mr. Bleach Blond actor dude there coming out of the arcade earlier, and I know Sprat stuck around for the skateboarding finals this morning, so it's no surprise he's still here either."

I nodded, realizing he was right. It seemed almost impossible that only a few hours had passed since the medical chopper had carried Cody Zane off that morning. But now that Joe mentioned it, I did remember seeing Sprat at the competition. It's pretty hard to miss a guy who's thin as a snake with spiky platinum blond hair. Especially one who's on TV every week. Sprat hosted his own show, *Gotcha*, on one of the cable music channels. I'd seen it a few times. It mostly consisted of Sprat and his buddies playing obnoxious pranks on other celebrities. Sometimes when they got bored with that, they'd build weird go-carts and race them until they crashed, or rig up public trash cans to blow up when someone dropped something in, or other similar types of stuff. It was all pretty juvenile, but oddly entertaining. I guess that's why it was a big hit.

McKenzie spotted us and strode over. "Where were you?" he demanded. "Took you long enough to get here!"

"Sorry, sir," I said. "We were just, uh, investigating something over by the entrance. So what happened?"

Sprat leaped forward to answer. "It was crazy, man!" he exclaimed, seeming more excited than upset. "We were all just chilling, testing out some of the planes and having a good time. Then all of a sudden, all the planes, like, freaked out!"

He waved his skinny arms around wildly. The other celebrities were all nodding along.

"Freaked out? What do you mean?" Joe asked.

"It was like they all, you know, attacked us!" one of the other celebs spoke up. I vaguely recognized him as an actor on a popular TV drama series, but I didn't know his name. "It was wild! I just hope the one that hit me doesn't leave a bruise, or my agent will have a cow."

McKenzie's scowl deepened at that. "Well?" he snapped at Joe and me. "What are you going to do about this?"

"First of all, we should probably see exactly what happened." Joe grabbed for the nearest set of controls.

"Joe, wait," I blurted out.

But it was too late. Joe twisted the power knob. One of the planes lying there, a model of a sharp-nosed Raptor fighter jet, suddenly came to life. It flew up, then started looping around wildly. I had to duck as it headed straight at me.

"Turn it off!" I shouted.

Joe hit the power again, and the plane crashed into the ground in front of him. "Oops," he said sheepishly. "Sorry about that."

I sighed. Mr. Impulsive strikes again. "Okay, it looked like that thing was trying to fly back at Joe, who was holding the controls." I walked over and nudged the Raptor with the toe of my sneaker. "My guess is someone is messing with the radio signal, redirecting all the planes to do that."

"Wild," Sprat said. "I'll have to try that on the show sometime."

McKenzie ignored him. He grabbed me by

the arm and dragged me a few yards away from the celebrities, who had started talking excitedly among themselves.

"Luckily, nobody was badly injured—this time," he hissed at me and Joe, who'd followed us. "But some of those boys got a little banged up when the planes hit them, and you know how whiny celebrities can be." He rolled his eyes, then stabbed a finger at each of us. "I need you to get to the bottom of this—now! Before it puts me out of business!"

It was obvious he was trying to keep quiet so the celebrities wouldn't hear him. But his voice was rising rapidly to its usual volume. Namely, *loud*. Most of the celebs were glancing over curiously. Plus, I noticed that a guy with a video camera had appeared out of nowhere. He was filming as they talked about what had happened. Great.

"We'll get right on it," I assured McKenzie quietly.

McKenzie sighed and rubbed his forehead. "Ticket sales are already down," he muttered. "If this gets out—well, I'm starting to wonder if it's all worth it."

He seemed to be talking more to himself than to us. "Don't worry, sir," I told him. "Joe and I caught the last two culprits. We'll get this one too. Just give us time."

"That's exactly what I don't have." He glared at us. But he looked a little calmer. "Keep me posted."

After he stomped away, Joe and I headed over to question the celebrities. Unfortunately, the arrival of the cameraman had turned Sprat into even more of a spaz than before. He was full of bluster as he postured for the camera.

"Whoever did this better watch out," he said. "If this is some lame rival show or something, I'll make them sorry they ever messed with the Sprat Man. If they want to mess with me, I'll mess them *up*!"

He swaggered around in a little circle, waving his hands. Half the other celebs were laughing and cheering him on. The other half were sort of backing away, looking anxious and muttering to one another. I thought I heard one of them say something about getting out before they "did a Bret."

In any case, we couldn't get much useful information out of any of them. Especially not without giving ourselves away to the cameraman.

"Maybe we should move on," I murmured to Joe as Sprat started boasting about how tough he was or something, getting right up in the camera and making faces. "We can talk to these guys individually later. But I doubt any of them knows anything."

"I hear you." Joe nodded.

We turned to leave. Just then we saw Ox Oliver hurrying in. "Excuse me," he said in a deep, rumbly voice. "I'll have to ask you all to step outside. I've been ordered to close down this attraction until further notice."

Sprat frowned. "Says who, man?" he complained. But when the other celebrities headed for the exit, he shrugged and followed.

Joe and I exchanged a look. I was pretty sure he was thinking what I was thinking. This was our chance to question Ox about the tractor incident.

"Excuse me," I said as we watched Ox string a chain across the entrance to the RCA park. "Um, we heard there have been a few accidents at GX today. Is this place, you know, safe?"

"Galaxy X is the safest way there is to live on the edge," Ox rumbled. "Everything is under control, and we hope you enjoy your visit." He sounded like one of the recordings that told park guests to keep their arms and legs inside the rides. I guessed that line was what McKenzie had told everyone to say if guests questioned them about recent incidents.

Joe cleared his throat. "Dude," he said. "Listen, you can square with us. We're just curious. What's the real scoop?"

Ox shot him a wary look. Then his expression cleared, and he smiled. "Oh, wait. You two must be the secret agents, huh?"

I winced. Great. Did everyone in the entire park know who we were now?

"Um, what do you mean?" said Joe. "We just heard—"

"Look, you don't have to worry," Ox said calmly. "I'm no snitch." He glanced at the celebrities, who were still gathered just down the path talking to the cameraman. "It's not like I'm going to give you away to any of those jerks with the cameras."

He seemed pretty sure about his theory. I decided we might as well give up and question him openly. "We just want to figure out if someone's still trying to sabotage this place."

"Do you know anything about the tractor that drove off the cliff-diving wall?" Joe put in. "Like, how it got up there in the first place?"

"You mean the one I'm supposed to drag out of the northwest lake?" Ox grimaced. "Yeah, I know how it got up there. I left it there this morning."

"You did?" I said. "Um, why?"

"Tyrone's orders." Ox walked over and scooped up several of the model aircraft in one meaty hand. "I got a text about it. Said I should close down the attraction and drive the tractor up there so I could do some work on that part of the grounds after closing tonight."

"So you drove it up and parked it?" Joe prompted.

Ox nodded. "Barely had time to get it up there before I got another text from the boss ordering me over to the other side of the park right away."

He sounded a little disgruntled. And no wonder. It sounded like McKenzie had him running all over the place nonstop.

"So Mr. McKenzie must be kind of tough to work for, huh?" I said.

Ox shrugged. "Tyrone's not so bad. Besides, the pay is decent, and I like being outside doing an honest day's work."

Just then a burst of rock music blared out over the park. There were speakers on all the lampposts, and they seemed to be turned up to full volume.

"Attention, everyone!" McKenzie's voice blared out as the music faded. "I'd like to personally invite you to a special presentation of the one-of-a-kind Galaxy X Super Stunt Spectacular! It's totally free, and it starts in ten minutes over at our fantastic open-air auditorium. So come on over and check it out!"

"Stunt show?" I echoed as the speakers clicked off.

Joe gestured to a kiosk just outside the RCA

park. Posters were plastered on all sides advertising GX's various shows and activities. "Must be that one."

I stepped over for a better look. Sure enough, one of the posters was for the stunt show. It showed stuntmen performing various death-defying feats straight out of the movies. A lot of them seemed to involve fire or explosions.

"Whoa," I said to Joe, my blood running cold. "If someone wanted to mess with things and make them go horribly wrong, this stunt show sounds like the perfect chance!"

Stunt Trouble

F rank and I said a quick good-bye to Ox and booked it over to the auditorium. It seemed pretty obvious that this special stunt show was McKenzie's way of distracting everyone from the latest trouble in the park. I just hoped it didn't backfire!

We got there just as the show was about to start. If I'd been a regular guest, the stunt show would've been awesome. McKenzie had hired a bunch of real stuntmen (and stuntwomen) from Hollywood, and they were totally amazing. They did all kinds of tricks, many of which I remembered from seeing them in the movies.

As it was, though, Frank and I spent the entire

time on the edge of our seats, watching for anything to go wrong. Several times I was on the verge of rushing to the rescue. Once when a motorcycle slipped off the high, narrow board it was driving over and crashed to the ground, I actually leaped to my feet. Frank had to grab my arm to stop me from taking off over the seats in front of us. Sure enough, I saw that the rider was parachuting to the stage, grinning and giving a thumbs-up. I covered up my mistake by letting out a whoop and pumping my fist, pretending I was just excited by the stunt. Luckily, nobody was paying attention to me.

Finally the show ended in one last blast of explosions and flamethrowers. When the smoke cleared, the performers came forward to take their bows. Whew! It looked like they were all still in one piece.

"Okay, that was a waste of time." Frank stood up. "Let's get back to work."

I nodded. "Should we go back and see Ox Oliver?"

"Nah. Since he knows who we are, he's not likely to tell us anything useful even if he is the bad guy. I think we should track down Nick. We still haven't talked to him about sending us on that wild-goose chase to the diving wall."

"Sounds good." I scanned the auditorium. Most of the guests were heading for the exits, eager to get back to the rides and activities. But a few people were standing in a group down near the stage. I spotted Tyrone McKenzie in the middle. Most of those around him appeared to be the remaining celebrities, including Sprat and the others from the RCA incident. "There's dear old dad," I said. "Don't see Nick with him, though."

"Big surprise there. I don't think those two hang out much, at least voluntarily." Frank glanced around. Then he blinked and did a double take. "Hey. Speaking of McKenzie's kids, is that Erica back there?"

I grinned and opened my mouth to rib him about his "girlfriend." But then I caught a glimpse of Erica and forgot all about it. That's because she was sitting sort of crumpled over in the last row—and it looked like she was crying!

Okay, that was weird. Erica wasn't the type of girl to cry because she chipped her nail polish or something. Nope, if she was crying, something had to be seriously wrong. And under the circumstances, that made me think we'd better talk to her right away.

"Come on," I said. "Let's see what's up."

Erica glanced up when we approached. She

sniffled and rubbed her eyes, looking sheepish and annoyed at the same time.

"What?" she blurted out.

"Are you okay?" I asked. "Why are you crying?"

"I'm not." Then she grimaced, realizing how lame the lie was, considering we were looking right at her. "It's no big deal."

"Come on." I sat down next to her. "Talk to us."

Frank stood there, looking sort of awkward. "We want to help," he added.

She shrugged and stared at her hands. "Like I said, it's no big deal," she mumbled. "It's just, this whole stuntman thing . . ."

If I were a cartoon character, a little lightbulb would've appeared above my head at that moment. "Hang on," I blurted out. "Your dad was a stunt-man, wasn't he?"

Frank's eyes widened. He'd obviously just remembered the same info I had. While researching Tyrone's family, we'd learned that Erica's father had been a stuntman. He'd died during a stunt gone wrong while shooting a video for one of the musical acts McKenzie produced. That was how McKenzie and Erica's mother had met.

"Yeah." Erica sniffled. "I didn't want to watch this show. But I couldn't resist, you know? I was so sure something would go wrong again, just like . . . well, you know."

I reached over and squeezed her arm. "It's okay," I said. "We understand. Right, Frank?"

"Uh—what?" Frank blinked. "Um, I mean, yeah. Of course we do."

Erica shook off my hand and stood up. "Thanks," she said, her voice quavering only a little. "Anyway, I should go. See you around."

She rushed off. I watched her go, then glanced at Frank. "Dude," I said. "You could've been a little more sympathetic. I mean, you know she digs you!"

"Whatever." Frank still looked uncomfortable. "It's not like anything I said would make her feel better. She lost her dad to a bad stunt, remember?"

"Yeah, that's my point."

Frank bit his lip. "Listen, I feel bad for her too. But we have a job to do, remember? Speaking of which, I had a thought about what Ox Oliver told us."

I could tell he was trying to change the subject. Typical. But I decided to let it slide. I'd been trying all my life to teach Frank how to copy my smooth touch with the ladies. At this point, I was starting to think it was a lost cause.

"What is it?" I asked.

"Why would McKenzie have Ox park that tractor up there and then call him away again?" Frank rubbed his chin. "Seems a little suspicious, doesn't it? Especially taken together with what McKenzie said earlier about the park maybe not doing so well . . ."

"Not being worth it, I think is how he put it." I nodded, forgetting about Erica's angst as my mind returned to the case. "Think we should go have another chat with ol' Tyrone?"

"Let's do it."

McKenzie was still hanging with the celebs on the other side of the auditorium. Frank and I hurried over. We arrived just in time to hear a hot young rap star complaining about all the trouble.

"Now I get why Kirk and the others left yesterday," he exclaimed. "Me, I'm out of here too, just as soon as my agent sends a chopper."

"Yeah," an actor put in. "I mean, I know Bret's death was an accident and all, but I'm starting to wonder about this place."

"I hope you won't let a few unfortunate incidents stop you from enjoying everything Galaxy X has to offer," McKenzie said. His voice sounded pretty normal, but the stress was showing in the form of a twitch at the corner of his mouth. ATAC teaches us to look for stuff like that. "In fact, if any of you would like to be my guests at a special video game party tonight . . ."

"No way, man." A popular NASCAR driver shook his head. "I read on the StopGX site that this might be only the beginning. Could be dangerous to stay, know what I mean?"

A few of the others let out murmurs of agreement. Then Sprat brayed out a loud laugh.

"Are you cats for real?" he exclaimed loudly. "I'm not afraid of what some lame website says! Even if there is someone messing with the place, who cares? GX isn't about being safe, is it? This just makes the danger seem more real—and makes the whole deal more fun."

Interesting. That comment almost sounded like something our old pal Sk8rH8r might say. Wasn't the whole anti-GX thing about the park trying to make dangerous stuff too safe?

"So you're sticking around?" one of the other celebs asked Sprat.

Sprat squared his shoulders. "Just try to pry me out of here," he said. Then he leaned toward McKenzie and smirked. "Well, as long as my visit is still comped, anyway."

Tyrone's mouth was twitching more than ever. "Of course. I'm thrilled to have you here as my guest for as long as you'd like to stay."

"Excuse me, sir," Frank broke in. "Could we speak with you for a minute?"

McKenzie almost seemed relieved for the excuse to get away from the celebs. "What is it?" he asked as the three of us moved out of earshot.

"We just wanted to ask you about those texts you sent Ox Oliver earlier," Frank said.

"What texts?" McKenzie was watching as the celebs scattered for the exits. "You mean about cleaning up the model planes?"

"No, earlier than that," I put in. "You know—about the tractor."

"What tractor? Oh, you mean the one someone dumped in the lake?" McKenzie scowled. "Yeah, I sent him a text to try to pull it out after hours. What about it?"

Frank shook his head. "We mean the texts before that. About bringing it up to the diving wall. And then the one afterward about coming over to another part of the park."

By now McKenzie was looking irritated. "What are you talking about?" he snapped. "I've only sent Ox two texts all day. I didn't tell him to park that tractor up there. Who told you that?"

"Uh . . ." I shot Frank a confused glance. What was going on here? Did this mean Ox was lying to us? Or could McKenzie be the one with something to hide?

At that moment a loud beep came from McKenzie's pocket. He pulled out his PDA and glanced at it with a frown.

So much for that interview. McKenzie almost always seemed more interested in talking on the phone or texting than he did in dealing with us face-to-face.

But this time he didn't mutter an excuse and walk away. Instead he read the message on his PDA and then held it out to us. His face was as white as a sheet.

"What is it?" I asked. Craning my neck to read over Frank's shoulder, I took in the text message:

YR STUNTS R FAKE JUST LIKE GX
MINE R REAL
READY 4 MORE?
—SK8RH8R

Too Many Suspects

"Well," Joe said, "guess that removes any doubt. There's definitely still someone out there messing with us."

Tyrone looked shaken. "This is an outrage," he fumed, shoving the PDA back into his pocket. "You two have been here how long now? And some psycho is *still* out there trying to ruin me! What was the point of bringing in ATAC, anyway?"

I didn't bother to point out that we'd nabbed two sets of culprits already. Was it our fault that a lot of people seemed to hold a grudge against GX?

"Don't worry, sir," I said. "We're working on it. I'm sure we'll have the responsible parties identified soon."

"You'd better." McKenzie glared at me. "Otherwise GX is doomed." He started striding back and forth in front of us like a tiger in a tiny cage. "There's not much else I can do to distract people and save the park's reputation. I mean, I've already pushed my crew to the limit to get Bomber Pilot ready to open tomorrow." He stopped short and glared again, including Joe this time. "Not to mention the new bunch of crazies weeping around over that singer, plus the usual old gang of crazies outside . . ." He threw up both hands and let out a sort of strangled roar. Then he stomped off without another word.

"Gee," said Joe sarcastically as soon as McKenzie was gone. "Think he's a little upset?"

We drifted out of the auditorium, stopping at a private spot behind a gift shop. "We'd better figure out what to do next," I said. "Let's go over the clues."

"What clues?" Joe rolled his eyes. "So far, just about the only thing we have to go on are those alleged text messages to Ox."

I nodded slowly. "Right. He says he got them, McKenzie says he never sent them. So which of them is lying?"

"Well, McKenzie's been on our suspect list all along," Joe pointed out.

"True." I leaned back against the gift shop's

back wall. "But we already know quite a bit about him. Maybe we should try to find out a little more about Ox."

Joe was already pulling out his phone. "I'll call ATAC HQ and get them on it right away."

While we were waiting for them to get back to us, we continued our search for Nick. We also went back to discussing Tyrone McKenzie.

"McKenzie's potential motive is starting to seem stronger all the time," I pointed out. "What if he's trying to shut himself down so he can collect some kind of huge insurance payout?"

"It's possible." Joe kicked at a rock in the path. "And he could've done most of the stuff himself, or paid someone to do it for him."

We hadn't reached any new conclusions when Joe's phone rang ten minutes later. It was ATAC reporting back on what they'd dug up on their initial check into Ox.

Unfortunately, there wasn't much to share. "Vijay says it's hard to find anything on this guy— almost like he never existed," Joe reported after hanging up. "Says they'll keep working on it and get back to us."

Suspect Profile

Name: Ox Oliver

Age: Mid-30s

Hometown: unknown

Physical description: 6'1", 225 lbs., blue eyes, bald, solid muscle

Occupation/Background: Currently head of maintenance staff at GX. Background unknown.

Suspicious behavior: Claims to have received two texts that McKenzie says he didn't send. Parked tractor atop cliff-diving wall for unknown reason.

Suspected of: Blowing up Mount McKenzie, causing tractor incident, other unexplained mischief at GX.

Possible motive: Unknown.

"Weird," I said. "Usually the HQ guys can give us a complete dossier on just about anyone within, like, thirty seconds."

"Yeah. Definitely suspicious. And despite what Ox said about liking the job or whatever, he doesn't seem too crazy about McKenzie."

I nodded. "Ox definitely has access," I mused. "He can probably get into any part of the park day or night without raising suspicion. Plus, as the go-to maintenance guy, it's a safe bet he's got the mechanical and technical know-how to pull off the stuff that's been happening—especially messing with the rides."

"So should we go talk to him again?" asked Joe. "Or keep looking for Nick?"

"Let's try to find Nick first."

"Good call. It still seems pretty suspicious that he sent us over to the cliff wall after Lenni when she was nowhere in sight."

We kept walking. "Although, come to think of it, Erica said Nick is hopeless when it comes to anything mechanical," I remembered as we neared the arcade. "So how could he pull off most of the stuff?"

Joe smirked as we both drifted to a stop. "Oh right, I'd forgotten about that. Then again, I'm not the one hanging on the lovely Miss Erica's every word."

I looked at him. "Focus, okay? My point is, we already know Erica knows her stuff when it comes to tech and mech—everybody says so, and we saw it herself when she juiced up that roller coaster. So if she says Nick can barely work his iPod, I tend to believe her."

"I see your point. But I still think we should check him out just based on the tractor thing. He could have an accomplice."

"Agreed. At this point it seems stupid to automatically assume that one person is responsible for all the trouble." I thought back over everything that had happened. "I mean, what if Nick set up that tractor stunt somehow to throw us off, but someone else entirely blew up the mountain—"

"Like Ox, maybe?"

"Sure, whoever. And then a completely different person could be behind the Leap and the RCA thing."

Just then I had to jump back as several people raced out of the arcade. They were all young girls. The tallest of them was clutching what appeared to be a life-size cutout of Bret Johnston. I vaguely remembered seeing it hanging on the arcade wall along with some other celebrity images. A security guard came chasing after the girls, shouting about getting them kicked out for good.

The whole scene reminded me of another potential suspect we hadn't discussed yet. "Maybe that Zana Johnston did some of it."

"The Bret superfan? I almost forgot about her." Joe watched the girls as they disappeared into the crowd, leaving the guard gnashing his teeth and reaching for his walkie-talkie. "Do you really think she could be behind any of this stuff?"

"Who knows? We don't know much about her.

The timing seems a bit off, especially for the explosion and other earlier stuff. Then again, we don't really know how long she's been hanging around this place. It's not like we'd have had any reason to notice her before."

Joe nodded. "She might've sneaked in early for the celebrity preview thing, or just come for the Mr. Nice Guyz concert or whatever." He made a face. "Although I'm not sure I'm with you on not noticing her. That kind of crazy is hard to miss."

Suspect Profile

Name: Zana Johnston

Original name: Zana Marie DeLong

Age: 19

Hometown: Silver Spring, Maryland

Physical description: 5'6"; 120 lbs.; long, straight brown hair; brown eyes; large Bret Johnston tattoo on one wrist.

Occupation/Background: Cashier and part-time college student; full-time Bret Johnston fan and founder of local branch of his fan club.

Suspicious behavior: Making various threats after Bret Johnston's death; openly vandalizing parts of the park in search of mementos.

<u>Suspected of:</u> Sabotaging GX.

<u>Possible motives:</u> To avenge death of Bret Johnston.

"Well, let's make a mental note to check into her if our other leads don't pan out."

"Speaking of suspects, I've got another one for you," Joe said. "What about Sprat?"

The loudmouthed TV star had been dancing around in the back of my mind too. "I hear you," I said. "It's like he's trying a little too hard to prove he's not scared of what's been happening, isn't he?"

"Yeah. Although to be honest, he's kind of the same way on his show. You know—trying too hard. But one thing's for sure—he's definitely an expert on stuff like explosions and tinkering with machinery."

I knew what he meant. Anyone who'd ever seen *Gotcha* knew that Sprat had a knack for that kind of thing. He was always hotwiring cars or creating goofy Internet scams or mixing together random stuff to try to make it explode.

"But what's his motive?" I wondered aloud.

"Maybe he's trying to drum up trouble to benefit

his show somehow." Joe sounded uncertain. "Or just get publicity for himself. Or who knows, maybe he's in with that StopGX crowd—if every teenage boy in America can come to GX and feel like they're living on the edge, it might cut back on the demand for his brand of shtick."

We had to stop discussing it for a while as we headed into the arcade to check whether Nick was there. For one thing, it was way too noisy for much talking. Besides, we didn't want anyone to overhear us. Even if at least half the staff seemed to know who we were, we were still technically undercover.

Nick was nowhere to be found in the arcade— or anywhere else in the park, for that matter. By the time GX closed for the night, we still hadn't located him. And when I called his house, the servant who answered the phone didn't know where he was and refused to give us his cell number.

By then Joe and I were back in the guest cottage McKenzie had provided for our lodgings. Joe sprawled on the couch, idly scrolling through the list of available video games on the console by the big-screen TV. "Strikeout," he said. "Guess we'll have to catch up with Nick tomorrow."

"Yeah. But listen," I said. "One thing keeps bugging me about all this. I mean, most of our suspects—McKenzie, Ox, Sprat, even Nick or maybe Zana—could've pulled off some or most of the bad stuff, at least theoretically. The Mount McKenzie explosion, the Leap malfunction, the skateboard thing, even the tractor. But you and I were standing right there when Erica got beaned by that rock. Wouldn't we have spotted someone as noticeable as Ox or Sprat or even Zana if they were hanging around at the time? Not to mention Erica's stepfather or stepbrother?"

Joe waved one hand. "I already told you, I don't think we should focus on that incident," he said. "It totally could've been old Freddy Jackson, or one of his protester buddies." He shrugged. "Besides, it's not like Erica was even hurt. Just freaked out or whatever."

"I guess you're right. Like I said, it just keeps bugging me, that's all." I shot him a wary glance, expecting him to start in on the Erica stuff again.

But he had a thoughtful look on his face. "You know, most of the people on our list can get into GX any time they want," he said, setting down the remote. "So what are we doing sitting around here just 'cause the place is closed?"

"Good point. Especially considering Skater Hater's latest message." I stood up and reached for a flashlight. "Let's go."

Soon we were wandering around in the semi-darkened park. Most of the neon lights and such were turned off for the night. But there were little safety lights on most of the lampposts and larger structures that let us get by without our flashlights most of the time.

"So what are we looking for, anyway?" Joe mumbled, stifling a yawn.

Good question. Sk8rH8r hadn't really given us any clues about where he might strike next. Not unless the stunt reference was supposed to be a hint.

"Maybe that stunt show is going to be the next target," I said. "There's supposed to be a repeat performance day after tomorrow, I think. And just because everything went smoothly today . . ."

"I hear you." Joe stopped in his tracks and glanced around. "What's the quickest way over there from here?"

We were standing in the shadow of the patriotic-themed roller coaster known as Old Glory. It formed the border between the military section of the park with the tank ride and others and the Wild Wild West area.

"I think it's this way," I said, pointing.

"Shh. Did you hear that?" Joe hissed, suddenly craning his neck to look upward.

"Hear what?" But before he could answer, I heard it too. Sort of a soft shuffling noise coming from somewhere overhead.

I glanced upward into the maze of metal tracks, but it was too dark to see anything. I reached for my flashlight and clicked it on, aiming up. . . .

Just in time to see an enormous undulating shape falling straight down at us!

Raging Rapids

"**A**aaah!" I yelped as Frank's flashlight beam showed something big hurtling down at us. I tried to run, but it was too late.

WHOOOOMP! I found myself enveloped in . . . fabric? I relaxed slightly as I realized that whatever had just fallen on us hadn't killed us. Not even close. Nearby, I could hear Frank thrashing and yelling. He's a little claustrophobic sometimes. I guess being attacked by a huge wad of cloth counts as one of those times.

"Relax, bro," I called, swimming my way through the fabric, looking for a way out. A beam of light shot through it—obviously Frank was still holding his flashlight—and I saw stars. No, literally. The light picked up a bunch of white stars on a blue background.

"Hey," Frank said from somewhere nearby, sounding a bit muffled. "I think this is a flag."

Of course. Now I remembered—the Old Glory coaster was draped in American flags of all sizes, including a gigantic one hanging off the side overlooking the park. Right over where we'd been standing.

A few seconds later we were both free of the flag. "Bummer," I said, nudging it with one toe. It covered a good ten square yards of the path and adjoining flower bed. "Isn't it, like, unpatriotic to ever let the flag touch the ground? Because this thing's touching a *lot* of ground."

"Someone must've cut the ties so it would fall on us," Frank mused, playing his flashlight beam over the side of the tracks up above. "Wait—did you see that?" He swung the flashlight lower, aiming it at a section of track just a few yards off the ground and a dozen yards down the path.

"What?" I squinted in that direction. "Hey! Is someone there?"

There was a scramble of feet on the metal tracks. Then a *thump* as someone landed on the path. Frank tried to catch the person in the flashlight beam, but whoever it was was too fast, darting into the shadow of the ride.

"Come on!" I yelled, almost tripping over the edge of the fallen flag as I took off after the person.

I had my flashlight out by now too. But our quarry was pretty quick, taking advantage of every snack shack, shrub, and oversize trash can to keep just out of sight. It was pretty easy to hold the trail by sound, though. GX was still and quiet, allowing every footfall to echo.

"I think we're catching up," Frank panted from just behind me.

I put on another burst of speed. By then I knew the lay of the land pretty well. We were crossing through a science-fiction-themed section at the moment. Unless our quarry changed course again, we'd soon be entering the picnic park, a grassy expanse separating the main area of GX from the back portion, where several of the more spread-out attractions were located. There were a lot of bigger trees and stuff there, along with picnic tables and volleyball nets. And, of course, the grass, which would muffle the sound of footsteps. That would make it easier for good old Flag Dropper to give us the slip.

There was one last clatter of running feet up ahead, then silence. "Hurry!" I cried, ready to burst out onto the picnic lawn and run for all I was worth. "He'll get away!"

"Joe, wait!" Frank grabbed me and yanked me a stop at the edge of the lawn.

"Let go!" I tried to shake off his hand, panting with exertion and eagerness. "He didn't have that much of a head start. . . ."

Frank shook his head and put one finger to his lips. At least I think that's what he was doing—it was still pretty dark.

"Shh," he whispered. "Just listen. It's our only shot."

I was practically quivering with impatience. I'm not exactly the type of person who likes to stand around waiting and listening. When something's happening, I'm ready for action!

But I realized Frank was right. We could run around the picnic park all night while our quarry slipped away into the darkness along its edges and disappeared. This way at least we had a chance. . . .

"There!" Frank hissed, pointing off into the darkness. "I heard something over that way."

I nodded, scanning my mental map of GX to figure out what was over there. "Could he be heading for the drag-racing track?" I whispered.

"Maybe a little more to the left," Frank murmured. "Sort of over toward that ride that hasn't opened yet—what's it called? The water one?"

"Whitewater Wipeout," I said. "Come on."

We tiptoed across the lawn, keeping our lights off. When we got closer to where we'd heard the first sound, we heard footsteps again. "One . . . two . . . ," Frank whispered.

Three.

"Stop right there!" I yelled as we both flipped on our flashlights, aiming them toward the source of the sound.

Like I said, our quarry was fast. All I could see was a blur of dark clothes as someone ran out of view, ducking under the barriers blocking the entrance to Whitewater Wipeout.

"Go!" shouted Frank.

I didn't have to be told twice. We both took off. I leaped over the barrier, hoping I was judging it right in the darkness. Beside me, I heard Frank skidding beneath it.

Even over the sounds of our running feet and heavy breathing, it was easy to hear a big splash ahead. "He's taking a tube!" I shouted.

"Guess that means there's water in the ride already, even if it's not open," Frank called back. "This could be our chance to catch up!"

The entrance trail led between some big fake rocks that hid the ride from the path outside. On the other side, some safety lights gave us a dim view of a rugged river tumbling rapidly downhill away from us. There was an equipment shack at the edge, and a bunch of huge inner tubes were sitting just outside.

"Banzai!" I yelled. Grabbing the nearest tube, I tossed it into the man-made river. The rushing water grabbed it and pulled it out of sight before I could even think about jumping on. "Oops."

"Quit messing around," Frank panted. He grabbed another tube and ran to the edge, clutching it in front of him. Then he sort of belly flopped in, landing facedown on the tube.

I followed suit with another tube. "Oof!" I grunted as I landed, almost slipping off one side as the waters spun my tube around. But I recovered quickly, wedging myself in and aiming my flashlight forward.

I soon picked out Frank's tube spinning along in front of me. He had his light on too and was scanning the rushing water ahead.

A stray current caught my tube and zipped me along faster than the rest of the river. I shot right past Frank.

"Whoo-hoo!" I yelled. Mission or no mission, this was fun! No wonder McKenzie was so bummed that this ride wasn't open to the public yet.

That—and Frank's yell of "Focus!"—reminded

me that this wasn't fun and games. My tube skirted the wall on one side, the rubber squeaking ominously against the craggy rock.

"Whoa," I muttered, kicking out and pushing myself away from the wall before a stray rock could puncture my tube. Guess that's where those still-missing safety barriers came in.

By leaning over and using my hands to paddle, I managed to get myself out of the side current and back into the middle of the river. Then I sat up and aimed my flashlight forward again as the water swooped me along.

"There he is!" I shouted to Frank, who was a few yards behind me now. "We're catching up!"

I tried to aim my flashlight for a better look. Maybe that way I could narrow down the possibilities of who we were chasing. After all, Ox was at least twice the size of Nick or Zana. . . .

Just then the river swooped around a sharp bend to the right and I lost sight of our quarry. I leaned over again, paddling with my free hand to try to push the tube along faster. I was so focused on catching another glimpse of the dark figure ahead that it took me a moment to notice that my tube had swayed out of the main current again.

"Aaaah!" I yelled as it careened straight into the high vertical stone wall. It bounced off again and hit a wave, jolting me off balance. I had to scrabble at the handholds to stay aboard. My flashlight went skittering out of my grip, disappearing beneath the water.

I gritted my teeth. That hurt. Now I had to rely on Frank's light and the weak glow of the stars to see our quarry.

A moment later I realized another disadvantage. It was really, really hard to keep track of where I was in the dark, rushing river. There was another alarming squeak as the tube scraped against some partially submerged rocks I hadn't even seen coming.

Man. In the daylight with safety barriers in place, this ride would be a blast. Right now? Not so much.

Frank's flashlight beam flickered past me. He was kind of far back by now, so the light was weak. But it was enough for me to see another bunch of rocks coming up dead ahead.

"Ack!" I yelped, leaning over to paddle, doing my best to scoot around the rocks.

I swooshed past them with inches to spare. Just as I was letting out a sigh of relief, the tube stopped short. This time it had banged up against the wall again. The current was strong here; it pushed against the tube, making it scrape painfully against rock as it continued downstream.

Reaching over, I shoved at the rough stone wall, trying to push away from it. I felt sharp edges slice into my hand. But it was like pushing against a mountain. The current was stronger than I was.

SKREEEEE—POP!

Suddenly the tube's taut rubber sides collapsed around me. Air poured out of its sliced-up edge, and I felt the current grab me, pull me out of the sinking tube, and slam me against the rock.

"Nooooo!" I yelled, before water filled my nose and mouth and the current yanked me under.

Flight Plans

"**J**oe!" I yelled as my brother's head disappeared beneath the roiling rapids. Luckily I'd had my flashlight on him when his tube went down.

My heart pounding, I used my hands and the flashlight to paddle. If the current swept me past him before I could get over there . . .

Whew! I managed to break loose of the main current. There was another current at the edge, even stronger and faster. But it carried me right toward Joe, whose head had just surfaced again.

"Heads up!" I yelled. "Grab my hand!"

Dropping the flashlight in the well of the tube, I leaned over the side as far as I dared. Without my light it was pretty dark, but I kept my gaze focused on the blob in the water that I was pretty sure was Joe. Then I stretched out my hand.

Yes! I felt Joe grab my wrist. "Hang on!" I called.

The current dumped us back out into the middle of the river. I hauled on Joe's arm, trying to pull him in with me. He grabbed at the edge of my tube with his free hand, doing his best to yank himself upward.

"Whoa!" I yelped as I felt the tube tip. There was a flash of light in my eyes, though it almost immediately disappeared. Oh, man. There went my flashlight.

But I wasn't too worried about that at the moment. Working together, Joe and I managed to get him out of the water and into the tube beside me.

"You all right?" I asked him.

He sort of burbled and gasped for a moment. "Yeah," he said at last. "I'm cool."

Those tubes are pretty big. Even so, it was snug in there with both of us. Plus, the extra weight slowed us down quite a bit.

"Lost my flashlight," I told Joe. "I don't think we're going to catch up to whoever that is up there."

"I know. Not like this, anyway." Joe sounded frustrated. "Think we could get this thing over to a spot where we could climb out?"

I looked over at the edge. The way the river twisted and turned to take advantage of space, it seemed possible we might be able to make it to the end of the ride on foot faster than someone on the river. Not likely—but possible.

"Worth a try, I guess," I said.

A sliver of moon had appeared by now, shedding some weak light over the landscape. We managed to paddle out of the current again and beach ourselves at a less steep section of the surrounding river wall. Good thing we both have plenty of mountain-climbing experience. Even so, we each almost fell back into the river a couple of times.

But finally we were out. "Come on!" Joe said, taking off across the top of the river wall.

I followed, moving as fast as I dared. Even so, it seemed to take a long time before we reached the point where the ride ended. Too long. When we got there, the safety lights showed us a wet tube lying abandoned on the beach.

"Oh, well." I slumped against a handy pillar, trying to catch my breath. "Guess we'd better call McKenzie and tell him what happened."

"You think Tyrone's new guards will be any better than that last batch he hired?" Joe asked the next morning.

I spit out a mouthful of toothpaste and glanced up at him. "Who knows? I just wish he'd listened to our advice to delay today's opening."

"Oh, come on." Joe rolled his eyes. "Delay the opening time? That might mean making less money!"

I snorted. The night before, we'd told McKenzie about our pursuit of the mysterious figure. He'd been concerned enough to promise extra security from now on. But he'd brushed off my suggestion that he hold off on opening the park until the place could be gone over thoroughly. The most I could get him to do was to agree to shut down Old Glory until the crew could check it out. He seemed pretty confident that Joe and I had chased off the would-be saboteur. But I wasn't so sure.

"He's just playing the odds, I guess," I murmured as I headed out into the main room of our cottage. "Never mind the danger to the public."

"Hey, that's why we're here." Joe grabbed his VIP park pass. "Let's get out there and sniff around before opening time."

Soon we were doing just that, starting with the area over near Old Glory. The more time passed without discovering anything suspicious, the more willing Joe seemed to agree with McKenzie's opinion that we'd interrupted the saboteur before any new harm was done. But I had an anxious feeling in the pit of my stomach.

About ten minutes before the gates were scheduled to open, I spotted McKenzie himself striding across the open area near the entrance. We put on speed to catch up with him.

"Excuse me, sir," I called.

He spun on his heel. "Oh, it's you two," he said. "Good work last night, boys. Let's hope you scared off that troublemaker for good this time."

"I hope so," I replied. "But I wouldn't count on it. Are you sure you won't reconsider delaying opening today? Just a few hours might give us enough time to—"

"Forget it," he cut me off, barking out a laugh. "Haven't you looked outside? There are more people than ever out there clamoring to get in! Who knew sabotage would be so good for business?"

I exchanged an alarmed look with Joe. "But sir—," I began.

"Save your breath, dude," Joe advised as McKenzie hurried off without seeming to hear me. "Tyrone McKenzie isn't the type of guy to change his mind if he thinks there's money to be made."

A few minutes later the gates opened. Tons of

people poured in, just as McKenzie had said.

"Check it out," Joe said, pointing. "It's our favorite crazy Bret fan."

I glanced over just in time to see Zana disappear into the crowd. "Guess she's back for more souvenirs."

"Or to make more trouble." Joe waggled his eyebrows.

"Do you really think she could be behind the mischief?"

He shrugged. "Who knows? I mean, I doubt she was the one who made Mount McKenzie go kaboom. But she could've done some of the other stuff."

Just then the PA system clicked on. McKenzie himself announced that the Bomber Pilot ride would be making its first run soon.

"Should we go check it out?" asked Joe eagerly.

I shot him a look. "We're not here to play," I reminded him.

He ignored me, taking off in the direction of the new ride. I sighed and followed. Why not? It wasn't like we had any leads to take us anywhere else. We had no idea where the saboteur would strike next. Besides, if McKenzie and his family were at the ride's grand opening, maybe we could finally talk to Nick.

Nick wasn't there when we arrived. But he was just about the only one. The little plaza around Bomber Pilot was packed. The only clear spot was a small roped-off area around the control hut, a tall, narrow wooden building made to look like an old-fashioned army outpost. There was a GX worker standing inside the hut. He was a sour-faced guy around thirty who was fiddling with the controls. Meanwhile McKenzie, Delfina (with baby), and Erica were standing in the roped-off area, along with Sprat and a couple of other celebrities.

Erica spotted us and hurried over, pushing her way through the throngs of eager GX visitors jostling for the best spots in line. "Hey," she greeted us. "Solve the case yet?"

"Not exactly." I felt a little weird—she was standing so close that I was afraid to move.

"Yo, Erica, is Nick around?" Joe asked.

She shook her head. "He's off-island today. Went over to the mainland to hang with some friends."

Bummer. Still, I figured it was useful information. If something else happened today, we'd know Nick hadn't done it. On the other hand, if things went smoothly, it made him a stronger suspect for the stuff that had already happened.

Over by the control hut, McKenzie was calling for attention. He welcomed everyone to the grand opening of the new ride, bringing a ragged cheer from the crowd. "And we have a special guest kicking off the inaugural run," he announced. "Sprat, come on over and get onboard!"

Sprat raised both hands over his head as more cheers came. "Dude, this ride is going to be a blast!" he shouted. "Let me at it!"

The GX worker had emerged from the hut by now. He stepped over and opened the door of the nearest plane-shaped car.

Sprat wrinkled his nose. "No way, dude," he said, brushing past the guy. "I want *this* one—check it out, number thirteen. Totally my lucky number!"

He hopped into a different car without bothering to open the door. It was bright red, with the number thirteen printed on it.

The ride worker scowled and rolled his eyes. "Thank you, Marvin," McKenzie said, hurrying forward and sort of shoving the guy aside. "Now come on—I'd like to personally show the rest of you lucky riders to your planes!"

Erica smirked. "Yeah, he'd better," she murmured to us. "That guy Marvin is kind of a jerk. If Tyrone wasn't so short staffed right now, he'd probably fire him. He's always acting like this job is beneath him."

"Really?" I glanced at the guy, who was still

scowling. "You mean he acts like he has something against GX?" I wondered if we might have another suspect to add to the list.

Joe didn't seem too interested. "You know, I bet McKenzie would let us go on the first run if we told him it was part of the investigation," he said. "Should we go for it?"

Erica laughed. "You totally should!" she said. Pressing up against my side, she smiled up at me. "I'd love to see you two up there flying around, being all heroic. Especially you, Frank."

I could feel my face going red. "Give it up, Joe," I muttered. "We have more important things to do right now than play pilot."

"Really? Like what?" said Joe. "It's not like we have tons of hot leads."

I didn't bother to argue. For one thing, he kind of had a point. Besides, McKenzie had just helped a couple of kids into the last available car, making the point moot.

"All set?" McKenzie called.

The riders cheered. Sprat let out a loud "Whoo-hoo!"

McKenzie hurried over to the control hut. He stepped inside and put his hand on the ride's controls, peering out the doorway. "One . . . two . . . three . . . liftoff!" he yelled.

The ride came to life. The central pillar started to turn, slowly and then faster. The plane-shaped cars started moving. As the ride went faster, they swung out on their heavy chains, flying around in a big circle. McKenzie stepped back outside to watch, allowing Marvin to go in and take over the controls.

"Check it out," Joe said, peering upward at the flying cars. "You can kind of see the laser images when they go past."

He was right. When I looked carefully, I could see that each car's screen made it look as if it was flying into enemy fire. Riders could use the controls inside to make the car zigzag up and down and shoot lasers at the screen images. To them, it looked like they were in a midair dogfight. To everyone watching, who could see the lasers but not the screen images, it looked like all the cars on the ride were shooting up each other.

"That looks pretty cool," I admitted.

Joe shot me a grin. "You mean we can give it a go on the next round?"

"Dream on. Maybe when we finish this mission, okay?"

"Aw, man. I always knew I got all the fun genes in the family, but this is ridiculous."

I looked at Erica, expecting her to join in on the

teasing. But she didn't seem to be paying attention to us anymore. She was staring at the rotating ride, a slight frown on her face. The ride was spinning faster than ever, the planes zipping around at top speed. The riders were whooping and hollering excitedly. Sprat's voice was audible over all the rest as he shouted in triumph with each laser hit.

"What's the matter?" I asked Erica.

She bit her lip, still staring intently at the ride. "I think something's wrong."

Before I could ask what she meant, she took off, shoving her way through the crowd toward McKenzie. "What's up with her?" asked Joe.

"Stop the ride!" Erica shouted. "Tyrone—listen to me! You have to shut it down right now!"

The last of her words were lost in a deafening metallic crunching and scraping sound. One of the cars overhead sort of jerked sideways.

"No!" I shouted, though I couldn't hear myself over the screams. I could only watch in horror as the plane-shaped car came loose from its chain and flew out over the terrified crowd. A second later it smashed into the control hut at top speed.

Dead Serious

"So what's the report?" Frank asked in a hushed voice. I clicked off my cell phone and pocketed it. "The hospital wouldn't tell me much," I said. "Sounds like the medevac chopper just got there a few minutes ago. That Marvin guy was DOA."

Frank grimaced. I could tell what he was thinking—we didn't need a doctor to tell us the GX worker hadn't made it. That steel car had totally demolished the control hut where he was standing. He hadn't had a chance.

"What about the kid who was in the car?" Frank asked.

"Sounds like he's going to pull through. But it'll

be a while before he's in any shape to hit the rides at GX again. Or, you know, walk." I shook my head grimly, glancing around. Frank and I were perched on a bench across the path from Bomber Pilot. Almost an hour had passed since the accident. The local police had cordoned off the ride with their yellow tape. McKenzie had also ordered the rest of this section of the park shut down. Frank had tried to talk him into closing down GX entirely, but he wouldn't even consider it.

"What a nightmare," Frank muttered. He looked over to where some police investigators swarmed around the downed car. "Wish we could check out the wreckage ourselves."

"Why bother? We don't need to know *how* it was done. What we need is to figure out who did it." Just then I noticed someone slumped on another bench further down the path. "Hey, is that Erica? We should go talk to her."

Frank nodded. "She was the one who shouted a warning. Let's go find out what she saw."

We hurried toward her. She was sitting there watching as a couple of guys with video cameras interviewed people about what had happened. Most of the park-goers seemed eager to recount their versions of the disaster—even the ones who admitted they hadn't actually seen it.

Erica looked pale and shaken. And no wonder. It's not every day you witness something like that. I mean, Frank and I have been trained to handle that sort of thing. And it was even pretty tough for us.

"Hey, how are you doing?" I said sympathetically, sitting down beside her.

She sniffled. "Okay," she said. "I just wish I'd noticed the problem sooner."

"What did you see, anyway?" asked Frank.

"It was the chains," she said. "Each car was supposed to have three of them. They're balanced to allow the cars plenty of up and down movement while still keeping them safely attached."

I nodded, impressed as always by her knowledge of all things mechanical and technical. "Supposed to?" I echoed. "Does that mean the car that crashed was missing a chain?"

"Sort of. All three chains were there, which is probably why no one noticed the problem. But once the ride got going, I could see that one of them wasn't attached to the car. I knew it wasn't going to hold up to that kind of force."

Frank reached over and awkwardly patted her on the shoulder. "It's not your fault. Someone should've caught that before the ride started."

"I know. But I still feel bad. I mean, Marvin wasn't the nicest guy in the world, but still . . ."

Erica sighed. "Anyway, I'm starting to wonder if it's true, if this place really is cursed."

I noticed that one of the guys with the video cameras had turned his lens on us in time to record Erica's comment. Yeah, McKenzie was really going to love seeing *that* show up online! Luckily, Erica didn't seem to notice. She was staring at her hands, looking bummed.

Just then Ox Oliver and a few of his workers appeared. They started shooing people away, setting up wooden barriers to close off the area.

Seeing him reminded me of our suspect list. Who could have done this? Was it Ox? He certainly had the access—and we still hardly knew anything about him.

There was McKenzie himself, of course. True, he'd barely missed getting taken out by that flying car. Or had he? What if he'd planned it that way to throw off suspicion? It seemed like a pretty risky stunt. We already knew that McKenzie was willing to take risks in business, or with other people's safety. Was he okay with risking his own life—and his family's—if the payoff was big enough?

If not him, then who? I had no idea where Zana was or whether she'd be capable of pulling this off. And of course, Nick had an alibi. Although now that I thought about it, being off-island today didn't necessarily let him off the hook. What if he'd set this up before leaving? Or what if leaving the island was just a cover story, and he was actually still hiding out somewhere at GX?

A *whoop* came from nearby, interrupting my thoughts. I glanced over. Aha. Speaking of suspects . . .

Sprat was a little way down the path, mugging for the cameras as usual. He didn't even look particularly upset, considering he'd just barely missed being in that defective car himself. Or had he?

Suspect Profile

Name: Stephen Pratt, aka Sprat

Hometown: New York, New York

Age: 26

Physical description: 5'9", 140 lbs., bleached-out spiky hair, hazel eyes

Occupation/Background: Started career as a stand-up comedian. Took on a variety of small TV roles before pitching and selling the idea for *Gotcha*, the weekly stunt show he now hosts.

Suspicious behavior: Always around when things go wrong; seems unaffected by tragic events.

Suspected of: Sabotaging GX.

Possible motives: Publicity, or unknown personal or business reasons.

"Hey," I said to Frank. "Sprat was awfully determined to get that one particular car on the ride, wasn't he?"

Frank caught on right away. "Think he might have known something was up with one of the other cars?"

Erica looked confused. "What are you talking about?"

Before we could answer, someone shouted our names. Uh-oh. McKenzie was barreling toward us. And he didn't look happy.

"This is an outrage!" he bellowed, skidding to a stop in front of us. "It's going to take some major work to get through this public relations disaster, I'll tell you that. I thought you two were going to put a stop to this sort of thing! What good are you, anyway?"

"Sir . . . ," Frank began.

McKenzie rubbed his head and sighed, deflating as quickly as a balloon that had just been poked by a pin. "Listen, I didn't mean to yell at you, son," he told Frank, his voice cracking a little. "I'm just upset, that's all. But listen, things are desperate— you've got to figure out who's trying to ruin me. What will it take to pull in more of your ATAC agents so you guys can get on this thing twenty-four/seven? Money? Just name your price."

"It's not that simple," said Frank. "We just—"

"Hold that thought." McKenzie's phone had just started ringing. He fished it out of his pocket and answered. As he listened to whoever was on the other end, all the color drained out of his face. "I'm on my way," he snapped, then hung up.

"What is it?" I asked. "More bad news?"

He didn't bother to answer. I'm not sure he even heard me. He was already striding away.

"Come on," Frank said. "Let's go see what's up."

Leaving Erica on the bench, we hurried after McKenzie. He headed straight for the park entrance. When we came in sight of the main gate, we spotted a couple of guards dragging someone out. Zana.

"Looks like she managed to snag another memento," I said, noting the chunk of wood she was clutching to her chest as she wailed tearfully at the guards. I'm guessing she was saying something about her dear departed Bret, though we were too far away to hear.

"Yeah," Frank said. "But why'd they bother to call McKenzie over for that?"

I glanced at the park owner. He wasn't even looking at Zana. His face was pinched with anger as he stared in the other direction.

I turned, following his gaze. "I'm thinking that's not why they called him." I pointed. "Look."

Frank's eyes widened as he glanced over and saw what I'd just seen. It was a huge banner hanging down from the nearest ride. I shook my head slowly as I read the message written in five-foot-tall letters:

XTREME SPORTS @ GX = SURFING IN A BATHTUB

"Whoa," I said, watching as a bunch of police officers swarmed toward the banner. It was still swaying a bit, indicating that someone must have just unfurled it. "McKenzie's not going to like that."

"Yeah, you're right," said Frank. "But at least a banner isn't going to kill anyone."

He had a point. Unfortunately, McKenzie didn't seem to share his relief. As we caught up to him, he was ranting and raving, sounding angrier than ever.

"This is it!" he shouted at no one in particular.

"It's the last straw. I can't take it anymore. Galaxy X was supposed to be a dream come true, but it's turning into a nightmare." He clenched his fists. "I'm ready to shut it down right now—for good!"

Familiar Chase

traded looks with Joe. Now what? Was
McKenzie serious about closing down GX,
or was this just more of his infamous tem-
per?

"Look!" Joe pointed again. "Is that someone up
there behind the banner?"

I spun around just in time to see a figure leap
to the ground beneath the banner and race off
into the park. The person was wearing a hoodie
with the hood pulled up, hiding his or her face.
But I had a feeling I knew who it was.

"Come on!" I cried, taking off after the figure.
"I don't think the cops even saw that."

The entrance to the BMX track was nearby. Our

quarry ducked inside, grabbed a bike, and took off down the course.

"Let's roll!" yelled Joe, brushing past the GX employee manning the equipment shed.

Soon we were on course, speeding over hills and taking jumps. It was actually kind of fun, though I did my best not to get distracted.

"Why does this chase feel strangely familiar?" I panted as I crouched over the handlebars, pumping the pedals as fast as I could.

Joe didn't bother to answer. "Lenni!" he shouted instead as we rounded a curve in the trail, coming in sight of our quarry again. "Come on, dude. Enough with the big chase scene, okay?"

The bike ahead kept going. But it slowed down a little. The rider glanced back over her shoulder.

"Are you guys alone?" she called.

"Do you see anyone else crazy enough to try to follow you?" Joe called back.

Finally she stopped. We caught up and jumped off our bikes. "Whew," I said. "You sure can ride."

Lenni smirked and pushed back her hood. "Yeah, I know. Pretty good for a girl, huh?"

She shot a look at Joe, who made a face. I hid a smile. He still hadn't fully recovered from the way she'd smoked him in GX's skateboarding competition earlier in the week.

"So it looks like you and your pals have been busy with the poster paint again, huh?" I said. "Nice banner."

She looked defiant. "Thanks. It's some of our best work. But what's with all the cops?"

"You mean you didn't hear?" said Joe.

"Hear what?"

We told her what had happened with the Bomber Pilot ride. Her eyes widened as she listened. Maybe she was a better actor than I thought. But she looked totally shocked, especially when she heard that a park worker had died in the crash.

"Whoa, that's hard-core," she said somberly. "I can tell you one thing. Nobody I know would do something like that. No way."

"Maybe so," I said. "But as far as Mr. McKenzie is concerned, you're suspect numero uno thanks to all the trouble you've caused."

"He can think whatever he wants. It wasn't me." She paused. "Hang on, though. Come to think of it, there *was* someone skulking around this place last night."

"Yeah," Joe said, leaning on his bike. "You."

"And us," I reminded him. "So was that you who dropped the flag on us?"

"Huh? What flag?" She shook her head impatiently. "Listen. I was up there hiding the banner when I heard what I thought was a guard coming my way. I ducked down and peeked out. Someone went jogging past, heading over toward the Western stuff or somewhere over that way."

I glanced at Joe. "Interesting. Did you get a look? Who was it? A guard?"

"I don't think so." Lenni played with a strand of her blue-tinged hair. "Whoever it was looked way too small to be one of Tyrone's thugs. I'm not even sure if it was a guy or a girl, but it was someone sort of slim and kind of average height."

That could describe an awful lot of people. I couldn't help wondering if Lenni was just trying to throw us off.

While I was trying to figure out the best way to question her, she blew out a loud sigh. "By the way," she added, "I assume you geniuses have already figured out I'm the webmaster of StopGX."

"What?" Joe squawked.

I blinked, both surprised and not by the confession. True, we hadn't quite put two and two together there. But it wasn't much of a stretch to think she'd be behind something like that, considering her grudge against the park. Plus, I belatedly remembered that she'd mentioned the site unprompted during an earlier conversation.

"So does that mean you're the one who's been sending us all those mysterious e-mails and stuff?" I asked. "You're Skater Hater?"

"No! That's not me." She shrugged. "I mean, yeah, of course I've seen that dude posting all around the Net. Even thought about banning him from my site—he seems pretty angry, you know? But I don't really know anything about him."

Just then we heard the sound of more bikes approaching. "Uh-oh," Joe said. "Sounds like someone's coming after us."

"See ya," said Lenni, dropping her bike and taking off into the landscaping.

"Should we go after her?" Joe asked.

"Why bother? She's already proved she can lose us if she wants to." I shook my head. "Do you think we can trust her? I mean, especially given what she just admitted about the website? That seems to be where a lot of the trouble starts."

"Yeah. Thanks to Skater Hater," Joe said. "But she claims that's not her." He bit his lip and glanced in the direction Lenni had disappeared. "Think she's telling the truth about the person she saw last night?"

"Who knows? Anyway, even if it is true, the only one of our suspects it lets out is maybe Ox. I mean, Nick isn't very tall, and neither is Sprat. It could still be either of them. Or that Zana chick. Or maybe even McKenzie himself, or some unknown person he hired to do his dirty work."

A park employee on a bike appeared over the nearest hill. "Yo, what's the idea?" he demanded irritably, skidding to a stop in front of us. "You guys too good to wait in line for your turn like everybody else?" He looked around. "Where's the other one?"

Guess that meant not everyone was onto our real identities.

"Sorry, dude," Joe said. "Uh . . ."

He was saved from coming up with an excuse by the ringing of his phone. He grabbed it and looked at the screen.

"Who is it?" I asked as the park employee glowered at us.

"Take a guess," Joe replied grimly, holding it out for me to see.

It was a text message from our old pal Sk8rH8r. This one consisted of a single line:

NEW HORRORS AWAIT IF U DARE!

Getting the Message

"**W**hat's that supposed to mean?" I muttered, staring at the message. Frank shot a look at the guy from the BMX shack, who still looked kind of annoyed. "Um, we have to go," Frank said. "Sorry, man. Didn't mean to cause any trouble."

He shoved his bike toward the employee. The dude reached out automatically to catch it before it fell. I caught on quickly, pushing mine that way as well. The poor guy was so busy juggling three bikes that he couldn't do anything but yell as Frank and I took off for the nearest exit.

Soon we were outside. "So did that text make some kind of sense to you?" I asked. "Because I'm not getting it."

"I'm thinking it could have something to do with Horror House," said Frank. "You know— that's the name of that funhouse type deal with the horror movie theme."

"Oh, right." Now I remembered the place. It was this big wooden house that looked like every haunted house from every horror movie ever. Supposedly a bunch of real Hollywood horror directors had consulted with McKenzie on it, and the interior was supposed to be super scary. I'd tried to talk Frank into checking it out on our first day at GX, but he hadn't gone for it.

We hurried over to the Horror House. There was a line of people out front waiting to get in. While they waited, they could check out the graveyard that covered the center part of the lawn out front. It was animated, so every once in a while a headless corpse or something would pop out and make everyone jump and scream and then laugh. There were also a bunch of other thematic decorations around, like a snarling dog peering out from under the porch, a bloody ax swinging from a tree, and a pair of mannequins done up to look like recent slasher victims lying beside the path.

"Check it out," Frank said, pointing to said slasher victims.

"Whoa." My eyes went wide. The two mannequins were lying there looking as bloody and lifeless as always. But someone had stuck pictures of different faces over their usual ones. "Is that supposed to be—us?"

"I think so."

We went closer. Yeah, once we got a good look, there was no mistaking it. Someone had taken a couple of fuzzy, bad, shot-from-a-distance-with-a-cell-phone-type photos of Frank and me, blown the faces up to life size, and stuck them on the slasher victims. The letters MYOB were written across the foreheads of each photo.

"MYOB," said Frank. "Mind your own business. Subtle."

"Yeah." I shuddered. It was pretty creepy to see our faces on bloody dead bodies. Even fake ones. "What kind of obsessive person would do that?" My mind popped right on over to the most obsessive person around—Zana the superfan. Could she be behind this? But why?

"Look!" Frank pointed toward the house. "There, in the window—is that Sprat?"

I spun around. Most of the windows on the house were boarded up, streaked with fake blood, or otherwise covered. But a few on the first floor allowed a glimpse inside. I was just in time to see a familiar head of shockingly blond hair moving past one of them.

"Yeah, that was him," I said. "Think he was spying on us? Maybe waiting to see how we reacted to this little stunt?" I glanced at the mannequins and shuddered again.

"Let's go find out."

We rushed for the door, flashing our VIP passes to skip past the line. Most of the people waiting gave us dirty looks or yelled stuff, but the employee at the door let us right past.

We entered the foyer. There was a body dangling from the chandelier and a bloody message—GET OUT!—scrawled on a mirror in blood. Deciding that probably wasn't meant for us personally—not that we would have paid attention anyway—I stepped forward onto a dusty-looking Persian rug. As soon as I did, there was a scream from upstairs, and a severed head bounced down the curving stairway and disappeared into a gaping hole in the floor.

"Cool!" I said, stepping forward to peer down after it. "I wonder if there's just one head that falls over and over, or a whole bunch? They probably have some kind of head return thing, like at the bowling alley."

Frank shot me an irritated look. I swear, the

dude has no sense of wonder or curiosity about the world.

"It looked like Sprat was heading this way. Come on." He hurried down a hallway off to the left. I followed. But the hallway was a dead end— literally. We rounded a corner at the end and found ourselves face-to-face with a bunch of chopped-up body parts.

"Bad call, bro," I said. "Got another guess?"

We went back to the foyer and tried a door going in the same general direction. It opened into a formal dining room. A bunch more dead bodies were seated around the table. A woman was facedown in her mashed potatoes with a butcher knife sticking out of her back. Another guy's bloody stump of an arm was dripping into a large soup tureen, while his hand floated in the soup.

"Nice," I commented as we hurried through. On the far side of the room was another door. This one turned out to open into a closet full of huge, hissing rats. I knew they were fake, but they sure looked real. We slammed the door shut again pretty fast either way.

We kept going, trying different doors and finally finding our way into the kitchen. I was expecting to find more murder and mayhem in there, but it actually looked pretty normal.

"Okay, which way now?" I asked, glancing at the three or four closed doors leading off the room. "It's not going to be easy finding someone in this—"

"AAAAAAAAH!" There was an unearthly scream, and a flaming, half-charred, screaming body burst out of the industrial-sized oven, heading straight toward us.

My ATAC instincts took over. I flung myself to the side, flattening out on the floor.

"Hey, cool!" said a new voice behind me.

I glanced up. A couple of park guests were staring past me at the charred corpse, which was already flapping its way back into the oven.

"Need a new pair of shorts, bro?" Frank reached down to help me up.

"Very funny." Feeling sheepish as I realized I'd totally fallen for one of the Horror House's special effects, I brushed away his hand and climbed to my feet. "You have to admit that was pretty good, okay?"

But there was no time to stop and admire the special effects. We kept going, stumbling around several more rooms and past more fake dead bodies. We finally caught up with Sprat in the upstairs hallway. He was checking out a body impaled on several broken railing posts.

"Hey," I blurted out, hurrying over. "We saw you in the window. Were you spying on us?"

Sprat stared at me. "Dude!" he said. "Why would I do that? I don't even know you, do I?"

"I don't know—do you?" Frank countered.

Sprat grinned sheepishly. "Okay, okay, you caught me," he said, spreading his skinny hands wide. "Are you going to kill me now?" He gestured toward the fake dead body. "Or I heard there's a torture chamber in the basement—maybe you can punish me there. You know, peel my finger-nails off or force me to listen to elevator music or something."

"We just want you to tell us what you're up to," Frank said grimly. "What's with the funny faces outside?"

"Funny faces?" Sprat blinked. "What are you talking about? I thought you were mad 'cause I figured out who you really are."

"Huh?" I said, shooting a look at Frank. This was kind of a strange confession so far. For one thing, Sprat didn't seem to be taking it seriously at all. Then again, from watching his show I knew there wasn't much he took seriously.

Sprat shrugged. "Look, that Nick dude told me you guys are, like, some kind of secret agents or something. So when I spotted you out there,

I was just, you know, checking you out."

Okay, that wasn't exactly the confession we'd been hoping for. "So you didn't stick our faces on the mannequins outside?" I demanded.

Frank elbowed me in the ribs. "Listen, Nick's full of hot air," he told Sprat. "Secret agents? Come on!" He laughed loudly. It sounded pretty fake even to me. Sprat didn't look too convinced either.

Still, we did our best to talk our way out of it, then beat feet as soon as we could. Once safely back outside, we huddled behind a handy mausoleum.

"So?" I said. "Think he's playing dumb? Or honestly clueless?"

"I don't know." Frank glanced up briefly as a huge black crow flapped out of the mausoleum and cawed at us. "I mean, he is one of our stronger suspects so far."

"True. We've seen him around for most of the pranks. Including the Bomber Pilot fiasco."

Frank looked thoughtful. "And we know he has the expertise to pull off most of the mischief. He's always building bombs and hot-wiring cars and stuff on his show."

"Yeah, he loves that stuff. We should definitely keep a close eye on him until we know more." I sighed, watching idly as the crow flapped its way back inside to await its next victim. "So I guess this leaves us right back where we started."

Frank nodded grimly. "Nowhere."

That evening McKenzie summoned us to come to his house and fill him in on the mission. "Got anything to tell me?" he asked as soon as we walked into his home office. "Such as why I shouldn't close this place down before it ruins me once and for all?"

"Well, we do have a couple of new suspects we're looking into, sir," Frank said. "For instance, our people back at HQ just e-mailed us some new info they dug up on your head of maintenance, Ox Oliver. They discovered that he used to be a professional stuntman, and—"

"Ox?" McKenzie shouted with laughter. "Forget it, boys. You're way off track. Ox isn't behind this trouble. Believe me, he's trustworthy."

"Are you sure?" I put in. "Because we really think he—"

"Tyrone! Are you home?" Delfina trilled, bursting into the room. When she saw Frank and me standing there, she giggled sheepishly. "Oh, hello, boys. Sorry to interrupt. I just wanted to see if Tyrone was ready for dinner."

Man. That Tyrone was a lucky guy. Delfina looked even hotter than usual. I remembered what Erica had said about her stepmother's appointment at the hair salon the day before and decided to take advantage of the inside info. I mean, yeah, I knew she was already taken. But it never hurts to practice your skills, right? That's a lesson Frank could stand to learn.

"No apology necessary, Mrs. McKenzie," I said with my smoothest smile. "By the way, you look particularly lovely today. Is that a new hairdo?"

"Why, thank you." Delfina touched her blond upsweep. "As a matter of fact, I did get it done yesterday. Although honestly, I'm surprised that Jean-Paul could do a thing with it, considering that little Tyrone Jr. was crawling around his feet the whole time!"

"All right, enough with the coffee klatch, people," Tyrone broke in impatiently. "If you boys don't have anything else to tell me, we all might as well get back to work."

I opened my mouth to mention our suspicions of Sprat. But it was too late. McKenzie was gone. Delfina gave us a little wave and hurried out after him.

"Guess we've been dismissed," Frank commented, heading for the door. "Let's get back out there."

Soon we were wandering through GX again. There was still an hour until closing, and the place was pretty crowded.

"Hard to believe McKenzie would even consider shutting down," I said as we walked along the main path, dodging hordes of park-goers. "It's not like anything that's happened is keeping people away."

Frank nodded. "It does seem strange that he'd suddenly be all over the idea of closing his cash cow. What did Erica call it that time? His baby, right?" He thought a moment. "Then again, what if that's been the real plan all along?"

"You mean this could all be some kind of big insurance scam or something?" I thought about that as we wandered down another path. "Guess it's possible."

A shout went up somewhere ahead. Suddenly a whole bunch of people starting rushing in that direction.

"Looks like something's going on," said Frank.

"Let's go see what." I took off at a jog, following the crowd.

We found ourselves swept along toward the auditorium. People crowded in from every direction. Once we entered, we could see the stage—every spot in the place had a great view.

"Is that Zana the Bret fan?" Frank said.

It was. She was up on the stage. Well, actually, she was up *over* the stage. Zana was perched on the metal scaffolding that held the stage's backdrop and overhead lights and stuff.

"I'm going to do it!" she cried out dramatically. "I'm going to jump. Life without Bret isn't worth living. I want to die in the same spot as my beloved!"

Tanks a Lot

"**G**rab the curtain!" Joe yelled, pelting toward the stage. I elbowed some curious onlookers aside and followed. Okay, so it wasn't too likely that Zana could actually kill herself by jumping from that relatively low height onto a wooden stage—if she even planned to actually follow through on her threat. She seemed like the overdramatic attention-seeking type to me.

Still, no point in taking any chances. Even if Zana just broke her arm or something, it might give McKenzie the excuse he was looking for to shut down. And then we'd never find the bad guy.

At first I wasn't sure what plan Joe had in mind. Then I saw him yank the stage curtain sideways.

He maneuvered it over beneath where Zana was standing.

Now I got it. I grabbed the other corner and did likewise. Now we had a fabric safety net beneath her, covering half the stage. Of course, if she truly wanted to harm herself, all she had to do was scoot over and jump down onto the other half. . . .

"Good-bye, cruel world," she wailed. "Bret, I'm coming! Aaaaaaaaaah!"

With that, she jumped. Or, rather, sort of toppled.

WHOOOMP!

"Oof!" I grunted as I leaned back, doing my best to balance the impact of her weight landing square in the middle of our makeshift safety net.

The watching crowd let out a cheer. "Is she dead?" some kid yelled. Nice.

"Guess it's okay to set it down now," Joe commented, letting his corner of the curtain drop. I did the same.

THUMP.

"Hey!" Zana complained, sitting up and brushing herself off. "You could be a little gentler, you know. Can't you see I'm in deep psychic pain here? I don't need a twisted ankle on top of that."

She didn't sound too grateful. Luckily, some guards and a medic rushed up to take over, saving us from coming up with a response. Joe and

I backed off and watched as the medic did her thing.

"You're welcome," Joe muttered sarcastically as Zana started complaining loudly about her twisted ankle. "This proves she's nutty enough to pull some of those stunts. But is she maybe a little *too* nutty?"

I'd just been wondering the same thing. Whoever was messing with GX was good. *Really* good. Most of the sabotage had gone off without a hitch, despite the fact that the place had tons of guards around 24/7. Not to mention Joe and me on the case. Could someone like Zana really pull that off?

We watched the scene for a little longer. Eventually Ox Oliver showed up and ordered the guards to escort Zana off the property.

"And don't let her back in," he added in his deep, rumbly voice. "As of now, Ms. Johnston, you're no longer welcome at Galaxy X."

"What?" Zana screeched, outraged. "You can't ban me! This is sacred ground! Blah, blah, blah!"

Okay, the "blah blah blah" part isn't a direct quote. But at that point her voice got so high-pitched that only dogs could tell what she was screaming about. A second later she grabbed a nearby microphone stand and swung it at Ox's head.

"Look out!" Joe shouted.

But Ox had seen the attack coming. He caught the mike stand easily in one meaty fist and wrenched it out of Zana's grasp. She collapsed on the ground, sobbing.

"I'd call that attempted assault, wouldn't you, boys?" one of the guards commented.

Another guard nodded. "Should be able to get her locked up for that," he agreed. "At least overnight."

"Take her away," Ox ordered, tossing the mike stand aside.

The guards grabbed Zana and dragged her off. By the time the sounds of her screaming and wailing faded away, most of the onlookers had dispersed. Ox was still there, pushing the curtain back into place.

"Come on," Joe murmured in my ear. "Let's go talk to him."

I nodded. McKenzie had seemed pretty confident that Ox didn't have anything to do with the sabotage. But Joe didn't seem convinced, and neither was I.

Ox glanced up as we approached. "Hi there," he rumbled. "You two the ones who caught that wacko?"

"Yeah," I said. "Just in the right place at the right time, I guess."

"So," Joe put in. "Is it true that you used to be a pro stuntman?"

That's my brother for you. Mr. Subtle.

Ox glanced up sharply. Then he quickly returned his attention to the curtain. He didn't say a word.

"Look." I decided to play good cop. "We don't mean to be nosy. It's just that a lot of stuff has been going wrong around here, and we're trying to figure out who might have a reason to cause trouble for Mr. McKenzie."

"Can't help you." Ox shrugged. "If I knew who it was, I'd deal with them myself."

"Really? Why?" Joe asked. "I mean, I know you like the job and all. But I bet you wouldn't mind seeing McKenzie taken down a peg, huh? Nobody would blame you for having it in for the guy."

Ox blinked at him. His expression seemed genuinely perplexed. "What do you mean?" he asked. "I don't have it in for Tyrone. He saved me!" Suddenly he scowled and shot us a look we'd seen plenty of times from suspects before. Joe calls it the oops-I've-said-too-much look.

I pressed on before he could recover. "Saved you? What do you mean?"

Ox just glowered at me for a second. To be

honest, it was a little scary. The guy is huge, remember?

Then he sort of deflated. "Look, you guys are secret agents. That means you can keep a secret, right?"

"Sure," said Joe.

"Okay, then it's true—I *was* a stuntman." Ox sighed, wandering away from the curtain. "At least until I got injured and had to quit. Had some debt and no other skills, and well . . . I pretty much hit rock bottom. Was living out of my car, the whole deal. Tyrone heard about it. I'd done some work for him back in the day and we always got along, you know? He loaned me some dough, gave me a job working for him and a chance to start over."

"Okay, nice story," Joe said. "But if Tyrone's such a great guy, why'd you look like you wanted to kill him yesterday?"

"What are you talking about?" Once again Ox seemed confused.

"It was right after the photo op at Bomber Pilot," I reminded him. "Remember? You were working the smoke machine or whatever it was."

"Oh, that!" Ox's expression cleared. "Right. Have to admit I wasn't feeling too happy just then. See, I told Tyrone we shouldn't try to open that ride yet. The crew finished things up in too much of a rush, the safety inspectors hadn't even had their final look at it yet. . . . There was just too much risk of an accident." He shook his head sadly. "Wish I'd been wrong about that."

Okay. By now I was pretty convinced that Ox wasn't our culprit. Beneath all that brawn, he was really a pretty nice guy.

"By the way," I said, deciding it was time for a change of subject. Even if Ox wasn't our bad guy, maybe he could help us. "We were wondering about that whole tractor incident. Do you have any idea who might have run it off the cliff?"

"Not a clue," Ox said. "Forgot to mention it before, but I had the start-up key in my pocket the whole time it was parked. Didn't want any guests coming across it and thinking it was part of the fun, you know?" He glanced toward some park guests wandering through the mostly empty auditorium. "So whoever did it must've hot-wired it."

Interesting. I traded a quick look with Joe, guessing he might be thinking the same thing I was. There was at least one person on our suspect list who was known for his ability to hot-wire stuff. Famous for it, actually.

We excused ourselves from Ox and headed back outside. "Think we should try to talk to Sprat again?" I asked as soon as we were alone.

"Definitely." Joe looked excited. "Let's go find him!"

"And fast," I added, glancing at my watch. "We don't have much time. The park closes in, like, half an hour."

We started searching. A bored-looking guard who'd just come on duty outside the arcade told us he'd seen some celebrities over in the Wild Wild West section. We headed that way at a brisk jog.

"Maybe that's him." Joe pointed to a small crowd gathered around the shooting gallery.

However, when we pushed our way through the crowd, we found that it wasn't Sprat who was showing off his skills. It was Erica. We waited as she sighted down the fake rifle, which shot lasers at a bunch of targets. She squeezed the trigger half a dozen times in a row, confidently and accurately taking out a cactus, several tin cans, and a fake cowboy's ten-gallon hat.

"Nice shooting," Joe said, stepping up as she lowered the gun to whoops and hollers from the watching crowd. "Where'd a nice girl like you learn to do that?"

I rolled my eyes. Joe never gives it a rest.

Erica glanced at him, not cracking a smile. "My dad taught me to shoot when I was little." She set the fake rifle back in its holder. "I try to keep in practice. I think he'd like that."

Even Joe didn't have anything to say after that. It was pretty clear that Erica wasn't doing this to impress Joe or the other guys. She'd done it for herself. And her dad.

"Last call, people!" the worker manning the shooting gallery yelled. "We close in ten minutes, so shoot 'em while you got 'em."

The watching guys started shoving forward and grabbing all the available rifles. Joe and I were shuffled away from the front along with Erica.

"So what are you guys up to?" she asked us as we found ourselves out on the cobblestone square that formed the center of the Wild Wild West section of the park.

"Looking for someone," I said.

"Yeah. That Sprat dude," Joe added. "Seen him lately?"

"Actually, yeah." Erica pointed at the area just across the square on the far side of the saloon. "He went past here a few minutes ago. Heading over there, I think."

"Thanks." There wasn't much time until closing, so I didn't waste any time heading the way she'd pointed. Joe followed.

"Hey," he said, glancing over his shoulder. "Your girlfriend isn't tagging along. Wonder if that means she finally realized what a loser you really are? Still, you'd think she'd want to come along and get to know *me* better. . . ."

Ignoring his babble, I put on a burst of speed. I'd just spotted Sprat outside GX's Western-themed bumper car attraction, which was called Whiplash. He was sort of dancing around, waving his arms at a young man in a GX employee uniform. Three other guys were standing there too. Two of them were minor actors, and the third was a popular VJ from one of the music channels. Guess that meant not all the other celebrities had left yet after all.

"There he is," I said.

Joe nodded, suddenly all business again. "Let's go."

We reached the little group just in time to see the GX employee shrug. "Sorry, dude," he said. "I can't let you on. I'll get in trouble. Each ride is supposed to be ten minutes, and it's less than that to closing now."

"Are you deaf, bro?" Sprat exclaimed. "I already told you, my friends here are leaving GX after today." He waved a hand at the other celebs, who all looked bored and indifferent. "They just want one last fun time before they split this scene, you dig?"

"Wish I could help you," said the employee, looking as if he wished anything but. "Can't do it."

"You could if you wanted to." Sprat glared at him, stabbing one finger into his chest. "You must be a hater, huh? Or a power tripper? Is that it? Does it make you feel cool to deny us big bad celebrities our fun?"

He was rapidly shooting past obnoxious to outrageous. I opened my mouth, ready to intervene. But at that moment the employee shrugged again.

"Whatever," he said irritably. "Just go ahead. But you'll only get a five-minute ride, okay?"

"Yeah, we'll have to play that by ear." Sprat grinned, slapping the employee on the shoulder. "Come on, guys. Let's roll!"

"Wait!" Joe called. But it was no use. Sprat and his friends were already racing into the bumper car arena.

"Never mind," I said. "We'll catch him when he comes out. He won't have anywhere else to go at that point—park'll be closing down."

We watched as the celebrities whooped it up on the bumper cars. They raced around, crashing into one another as hard as they could.

"No wonder they call it Whiplash," I commented, wincing as Sprat slammed into one of the others with a howl of triumph.

"Yeah," said Joe eagerly. "It looks like fun! Maybe we should hop in too—you know, try to talk to Sprat while we're out there. . . ."

I shot him a look. "Nice try, bro."

We kept watching. And watching. And then watching some more. Way more than five minutes passed—more like twenty. Finally I glanced at the employee. He was standing outside the control hut, looking disgruntled.

"I wonder why he's not shutting them down," I said. "Even if he doesn't control the individual cars, there must be some kind of override button for emergencies."

"Maybe he called McKenzie to let him know what was happening." Joe suggested. "McKenzie might've told him to go ahead and let them have their fun."

"Could be." I smirked. "Looks like the employee's having his own fun, though. He isn't bothering to turn on the lights." I'd noticed it was getting darker and darker out there. If it wasn't for the lines of running lights along the bottom of each bumper car, we'd barely be able to see them at all soon.

"Yeah," Joe said wistfully. "Bumper cars in the dark—how cool is that?"

I leaned back against a handy railing, ready to wait as long as it took for Sprat and his friends to finally get tired of the game. Meanwhile I started turning over the case in my mind. Something about it wasn't sitting quite right, though I wasn't sure what or why. It was just a funny little feeling. Like there was a clue right in front of our faces; something we'd missed . . .

CRRRRUNCH!

The ear-shattering noise of metal crunching over splintering wood yanked me out of my thoughts. "What's that?" I cried, whirling toward the source of the sound.

Joe and the GX employee were already staring that way. "Whoa!" Joe shouted. "It's a tank!"

He was right. Even in the darkness, it was easy to see the enormous metal tank as it crashed through the wall separating the bumper cars from the attraction next door. The top was flipped open, making it obvious that there was no one inside controlling the thing as it rumbled forward, bearing down on the bumper cars.

"Look out!" one of the celebrities cried, steering his car out of the way. "Sprat, it's coming right at you!"

Sprat was trapped in a corner of the arena. He tried to steer away, but it was too late—a couple of empty bumper cars were blocking his only escape route. He cowered in his bumper car, staring up in fear as the tank rumbled toward him.

In the Dark

"**G**et out!" I shouted, racing toward the edge of the arena. "Sprat, you've got to run for it!" That seemed to snap Sprat out of his terror. He pushed himself out of the car, almost tripping over the edge.

"Go! Go!" the GX employee yelped.

Sprat caught himself and leaped over the other empty cars. His foot caught inside one of them and he started to trip again. I winced, glancing at the tank. It was almost on him by now. Could he make it? Or were we going to see him crushed in front of our eyes?

"Aaaaaaah!" Sprat howled, shoving himself back to his feet and making one last wild leap over the remaining car. He landed hard but stayed upright, sprinting out of the way just as the tank crunched over the front edges of the cars. Seconds later it crashed into the padded cement wall and finally came to a stop.

"Whoa!" one of the other celebrities exclaimed as Sprat staggered toward us. "That was close, dude!"

Yeah. Too close. "Come on," Frank said to me. "Let's check out that tank."

We raced over. "Think someone could be crouched down inside?" I panted.

"We'll see."

But when we climbed up the side and peered in, we saw that everything was just as it appeared. The cockpit of the tank was empty.

"Hang on," said Frank, pointing. "What's that?"

I squinted, trying to see in the darkness. Then I spotted it. A stick was wedged into the controls, keeping them on Full Speed Ahead.

"Yeah. This was no accident," I said grimly. "Looks like our saboteur has struck again."

Frank glanced over his shoulder toward Sprat. "And it kind of looks like it wasn't you-know-who."

"Good point. Think we should go check out the tank attraction?"

"Guess so." Frank shrugged. "But no hurry. I doubt our culprit is hanging around over there waiting to get caught."

He had a point. So we headed back over to see if Sprat was okay. He'd recovered from his ordeal by now—or at least his mouth had. He was ranting and raving about GX being a death trap. At least that was the gist of it.

"This is supposed to be a safe place to have fun!" he was yelling as we joined the crowd around him, which was growing by the second. The park was officially closed by now, but a lot of stragglers and GX employees must have heard the commotion.

"Uh-oh," I breathed into Frank's ear. "Tyrone's not going to be happy when he finds out about this."

He nodded, glancing over at Erica, who'd just joined the group. She had her cell phone pressed to her ear and a serious look on her face. "Unless I miss my guess," he said, "he's finding out right now."

Sprat was still ranting. "Just wait until my publicist gets hold of this!" he yelled, jabbing his finger in the hapless employee's face. "Let alone my fans! What are they going to say when they hear I almost got killed?"

The dude had a point. I could only imagine the

public outcry. Especially if Sprat blabbed to every TV show and fan magazine around.

For a second I wondered if Sprat could be behind this latest stunt after all. What if he'd set it up to throw suspicion off himself?

I dismissed the theory almost as soon as it formed. No way would a guy like Sprat make himself look like a terrified mess. He'd probably rather go to jail than that.

That gave me an idea. I shoved my way forward.

"Yeah," I said loudly. "You're right, dude. Everyone should know about this incident."

Sprat shot me a look. "Right. That's what I'm saying, bro."

"I hear you." I widened my eyes, trying to look as supportive as possible. "I mean, living on the edge is one thing. But scaring people to death? Not cool, man." All eyes were on me by now. "And that must've been pretty scary to make a guy like you scream like a girl the way you did."

There was a soft snicker from somewhere nearby. I was pretty sure it was one of the other celebs.

"My brother's right." Frank caught on fast. "And don't worry, we were watching the whole thing. We can totally describe everything that happened to anyone who asks. *Everything*."

I hid a smile as I caught the look of dawning comprehension on Sprat's face. So much for that fearless, death-defying bad-boy image he'd built up on his show . . .

By now the employee from the ride had caught on as well. "Me too," he spoke up. "You know, I had my cell phone out when it happened. It has a recording thingy. I might even have caught that scream on it. If I'm lucky."

"Dude!" one of the other celebs said with a laugh. "You've totally got to put that on VideoUp.com!"

Erica nodded. "Tyrone always says any publicity is good publicity, right?" she put in. Guess she'd caught on too.

"Forget it," Sprat muttered as a few other onlookers started laughing. "I was just playing, you guys. Can't believe you fell for it. Actually, facing down that tank was kind of a rush." He shrugged. "Anyway, I'm out of here. It's late, and I've got better things to do than give Tyrone even more free publicity for this lame place."

"I could hardly keep from busting out laughing when Sprat went slinking away like that," I chortled.

"Yeah, well don't get too happy about that." Frank glanced up from his laptop. "With Sprat out of the picture, our suspect list is shrinking fast."

An hour or so had passed since Tank vs. Bumper Car. We'd thought about hanging around out there after closing. But McKenzie had every extra guard on duty, so there didn't seem much point.

So now we were back in the guest cottage, discussing the mission. Not that there was much to discuss. Frank was right—our suspects were dropping like flies.

"Okay, so we're both convinced that Ox is innocent, right?" I said.

Frank nodded. "It's still weird about those text messages from Tyrone," he said. "But after talking to Ox, I just don't think he'd do most of that stuff. Besides, that person Lenni spotted was too small to be him, remember?"

"Good point. It could've been Sprat, but then again, he couldn't have rigged that tank while he was over at the bumper cars." I leaned back against the couch cushions. "Although I suppose it's possible the tank thing wasn't connected to the others. Maybe someone had it out for Sprat or one of those other guys?"

"Maybe." Frank didn't sound convinced. "But by that token, Zana would still be in the picture too. She was in jail for this latest thing, but not the others."

"Yeah. But she was always kind of a weak suspect anyway." I chewed my lower lip. "So let's just say she's out, Sprat's out, Ox is out—who's left?"

"McKenzie himself. He's always been on the list." Frank thought a moment. "And if we asked him for his input, he'd still probably say Lenni."

"And then there's Nick," I added. Then I paused. "Or wait—maybe not. Didn't Erica say he was going to be on the mainland all day?"

"Yeah. But unless she's got a GPS on him, he could've sneaked back over, or maybe never gone at all. Either way, it's past time for us to talk to him." Frank bent over his laptop, his fingers flying over the keyboard. "There," he said after punching one last button. "I just sent him an e-mail saying we need to talk to him in the morning."

"Cool." I stood up and stretched. It had been a long day. "Then let's hit the sack. Not much else we can do until then."

FRANK

15

Painted into a Corner

When I woke up the next morning, the first thing I did was check my e-mail. There was a message waiting from Nick.

"Get up, Joe." I nudged my brother, who was still conked out and drooling on his pillow. "We've got to move."

"Wha—huh?" Joe rolled over, cracked one eye open, and gazed at me blearily. He's not much of a morning person.

"Nick wrote back." I grabbed Joe's shorts off the end table and tossed them at him. "He wants to meet us at eight."

Joe sat up and rubbed his eyes. "But GX doesn't even open until nine," he complained.

"I know. We're meeting up at the paintball place. Nick says he's been dying to try it out and doesn't want to deal with the public."

"That sounds like him." Joe yawned and pulled on his shorts. He was looking a little more awake already. "And hey, paintball sounds cool. Maybe we can give it a whirl while we're at it."

I didn't bother to remind him that we weren't there to have fun. "Hurry up," I said instead. "It's already quarter till."

At exactly three minutes to eight, we were stepping out the door. We'd only gone a short way down the path when we spotted someone ahead of us.

"Hey, there's Nick now." Joe cupped his hands around his mouth. "Dude! Wait up!"

When we caught up, Nick looked less than thrilled to see us. "What do you want?" he snapped.

I was a little surprised by the attitude. I figured maybe he wasn't a morning person either.

"We were just on our way to meet you." I chuckled. "Guess you're running late too, huh?"

He stared at me. "What are you talking about?"

"What do you mean, what are we talking about?" Joe rolled his eyes. "You were the one who wanted to meet up at paintball this morning, remember?"

"Huh?" Nick looked perplexed and kind of irritated. "Listen, I'm not in the mood for your little secret-agent games right now, okay?"

I traded a look with Joe. "Hang on," I said. "Are you saying you didn't reply to our e-mail this morning?"

"What e-mail? I haven't even logged on yet today."

Okay, this was weird. If Nick hadn't sent that e-mail, who had? Still, I figured we might as well question him before he disappeared on us again.

"Hey," I said. "We've been wanting to ask you about something. How'd you know Lenni was over at the cliffs the other day?"

"Lenni who?"

"You know. The skater chick," Joe put in. "Blue hair? Ring a bell?"

"Oh, her." Nick shrugged. "Wait, what cliffs?"

"You came over to us," I said with as much patience as I could muster. "Said you'd seen her making trouble over at the cliff-diving wall. Day before yesterday."

"Oh, wait." Finally he seemed to have some clue what we were talking about. "Yeah, I remember. But I didn't see her myself or anything. Just heard about it."

"From who?" asked Joe.

Nick shrugged again. "I don't know. My dad, maybe? Or was it Erica? Oh, wait—it could've been that guy Sprat. I hung with him from a while that day."

We tried to get him to remember more. But he seemed to be getting impatient with the whole conversation. Finally he muttered an excuse—something about Delfina and Tyrone Jr.—and took off.

"So much for that," Joe said, watching him go. Then he glanced at me. "Think we should keep our date with 'Nick' at the paintball place?"

"Definitely." I grinned as things finally settled into place in my mind. Why hadn't I seen it before? "And I'm pretty sure I just figured out who's going to be waiting for us there," I added, quickly filling him in on my thoughts.

When I finished, Joe let out a whistle. "Bro, you are good!" he said. "But hang on—I think we forgot something we might need." He turned to head back toward our cottage.

"Got your phone on you?" I called after him.

Joe paused and fished out his phone. He tossed it to me. "Be right back."

"What a surprise. Nobody waiting to meet us," Joe murmured as we carefully entered the paintball office a few minutes later.

"Yeah. But somebody's expecting us. Look."

I pointed to the door leading into the rest of the attraction. It was closed, and someone had tacked up another blurry photo of the two of us there. Typed at the top of the page was a message:

I WARNED U. LAST CHANCE 2 MYOB.
—Sk8rH8r

"Now I feel totally welcome," Joe quipped. "Come on, let's get suited up."

Soon we were pushing through the door, paintball guns at the ready. We were dressed in baggy white suits and helmets with face shields. The interior of the warehouselike paintball course was dark and still.

"Hit the lights," I whispered to Joe.

He reached over and felt along the wall. There was the sound of a flipping switch. But nothing happened.

"No luck," he whispered.

No surprise there. Sk8rH8r wasn't going to make this easy.

All my senses were on high alert as we tiptoed farther in. Just enough light seeped in around the edges of the shaded windows to let us see big, blobby shapes all around us. Bunkers and other obstacles. But wait—was that one moving?

I tensed, gripping my paintball gun tighter. After a second, I realized my eyes were playing tricks on me. It was just another bunker. I relaxed slightly and took another step.

"This place is awesome!" Joe whispered from just behind me.

"Shh!" I hushed him. "The more noise we make, the more likely—"

My next words were lost in the blast of gunfire. "Duck!" I shouted, hitting the floor as the shot whizzed overhead.

Joe dodged behind a bunker. "Come on!" he yelled. "Let's run for the next one—we should be able to see more from there."

I glanced behind me, trying to gauge what kind of velocity the paintballs were carrying. We'd figured Sk8rH8r was going to rig up the gun to make those paintballs hurt if they hit us—probably a lot. But my eyes widened as I located the spot where the shot had landed. Even in the dark, I didn't like what I saw.

"Get down!" I shouted at my brother. "That's not a paintball gun—it's a real one!"

But it was too late. Joe was already sprinting for the next bunker.

The unseen shooter fired again.

"Aaaaah!" Joe howled in pain as the shot hit him straight in the chest and flung him back against the wall.

Last Shot

I was in a world of hurt. But I managed to roll to one side to avoid the next shot. Meanwhile Frank let out a shout and sprinted forward. He disappeared between two bunkers, and a muffled cry went up.

I squeezed my eyes shut against the pain. When I opened them, a huge figure was looming over me.

"Ox," I gasped out. "Is—is that you?"

"It's me." He leaned closer, reaching toward me. "You still with us?"

"I'm okay—go help Frank."

Ox nodded and ran. He moved fast for such a big guy.

"Gotcha!" he shouted a moment later.

I managed to sit up as he and Frank reappeared. Between them, struggling against their grip, was Erica.

"Let me go!" she sobbed. "It's not my fault! I told you to back off, and you just wouldn't. . . ."

I pushed myself to my feet. I have to admit it—it hurt. A loud groan escaped before I could stop it. "Ow, that smarts," I muttered.

Erica heard me. Her head whipped around and her eyes went wide. "You—but I thought I—," she stammered in shock.

Shaking off the last bit of wooziness, I peeled back my protective suit. That revealed the bullet-proof vest underneath. Standard ATAC issue from our kits. Frank was wearing his, too.

Yeah, that was what I'd gone back inside to get before we came over. Although I have to admit, I never thought it would have to deflect actual, you know, *bullets*. I'd just figured, better safe than sorry. I'd been paintballing before, and those things can hurt when they hit you, even at normal speed. With Erica's talent for rigging stuff, I'd expected some supersonic paintballs coming our way. Besides, we hardly ever got to use those vests, so what the heck?

"Okay, now I'm really, really glad I went back

for these," I said, wincing as I peeled the vest away from my sore chest. "Although I wish the HQ guys had told us it still hurts like crazy when you get shot."

"Consider the alternative, bro," Frank advised.

Erica was still sobbing. She'd gone kind of limp. Frank let go, though Ox kept his grip on her arm.

"Glad we called you, too," Frank told Ox. "She was really putting up a fight when I caught up to her." He pushed back his face guard and touched a spot just below where it had extended. "That one punch is definitely going to leave a bruise."

"Glad to help," Ox rumbled. Then he pulled out his cell phone with his free hand and punched in a number.

"I didn't mean to hurt anyone," Erica wailed as Ox murmured in low tones to the person on the other end of the line. "I swear. I only used birdshot—it was just supposed to scare you off."

"Right." Frank glared at her. "And what if it had hit one of us in the face? That would've been pretty scary, all right."

"Are you kidding?" She sniffled and glared back, looking defiant. "You've seen me shoot. I never miss."

"So why'd you do it?" I asked, limping over to

her. "I mean, my brilliant brother here figured out it was you—"

"It had to be," Frank put in. "She had the technical know-how to pull off all the tricks—the bombs, redirecting those model planes, rigging the tank and tractor, the whole deal." He paused. "But I still didn't put two and two together until something finally clicked. It was bothering me for a while, actually—that feeling we were missing something. It was what Delfina said yesterday when you started up with the lame flirting—"

"Hey!" I protested, touching the sore spot on my chest. "A little respect for the wounded, okay?"

Frank rolled his eyes. "Anyway, you mentioned her new hairstyle, and Delfina mentioned that Tyrone Jr. was with her at the hair salon. But Erica here had claimed she was stuck at home babysitting him all day while stepmom got her hair done—the same day that we almost got taken out by that runaway tractor." He snapped his fingers. "Busted alibi."

I nodded. He'd already filled me in—at least the basics—outside the cottage. But Ox looked intrigued.

"But why?" he asked, glancing at Erica. "Why would you want to ruin this place? Your father's dream?"

"He's not my father." She still looked defiant. "But I don't have to tell you anything. I want a lawyer."

We kept trying. But she was stubborn. She wouldn't say a word—until the door burst open and Tyrone stormed into the room. That's who Ox had called.

"What's going on here?" he thundered.

That's when Erica freaked out. "This is all your fault!" she screamed, twisting loose from Ox and racing toward her stepfather. "Everything's your fault!"

She leaped at him, pummeling him and clawing at his face. It took all three of us to peel her off of him, and by the time we did he was sporting several deep scratches thanks to her fingernails. He touched a finger to one and swore as he drew it back with blood on it.

"Whoa!" said Frank as Ox finally got Erica under control with her hands behind her back. "Okay, I'm guessing this has something to do with you, Mr. McKenzie. . . ."

"It has everything to do with him!" Erica spat out, still struggling against Ox. "He killed my real dad!"

Huh? Everyone was confused at first. But as Erica kept ranting, we started to figure it out.

Erica blamed McKenzie for her real father's death because the stunt he was doing when he died was for one of McKenzie's music videos. Okay, that didn't make much sense. But if there was one thing working for ATAC had taught me, it was that bad guys—or girls, in this case—weren't always rational about why they did what they did.

Anyway, it seemed Erica was still harboring some major resentment against ol' Tyrone, whether he was actually responsible or not. It didn't help much that he'd first married and then dumped her mother, either. Besides that, it sounded as if he'd barely noticed that Erica existed until he had to— namely, when her mother died while Erica was still a minor. She hadn't had any other close family, and so he'd taken her in.

"But it was obvious you never wanted me around," she spat out, shooting daggers with her eyes. "I'm sure the only reason you didn't throw me in foster care or something was to avoid any bad publicity."

I glanced over at McKenzie, expecting him to deny that. But he just shrugged. "Go figure," he said, dripping sarcasm. "Can't imagine why anyone wouldn't want such a lovely stepdaughter around."

Harsh. But now Erica's motive was looking

pretty obvious. When she'd seen how excited her stepfather was about GX—his "baby," as she herself had put it—she'd seen her chance for a little revenge. It had started with some online agitating as Sk8rH8r, and she claimed that at first that was all she'd planned to do.

But then Frank and I got sent in to investigate the online threats—and the other early vandalism, which wasn't her doing—and she panicked. That was why she'd faked getting hit by that rock. She was trying to throw us off in case we suspected her.

"See?" Frank glanced at me when she admitted that part. "I knew that was an important clue. I just never figured out what it meant, that's all."

I nodded. "And then things escalated even more, right?" I said to Erica.

"I guess." By now she actually seemed eager to talk. Maybe she wanted her stepfather to know exactly how deep her grudge ran. "Anyway, that old geezer and his nephew kind of inspired me, I guess. I mean, their stunts were good—but I knew I could do a lot better." She actually smirked as she shot another look at McKenzie. "Like blowing up that stupid mountain. You shouldn't have called it Mount McKenzie, Tyrone. Why not just name it what it was—Mount Ego?"

"Why, you—" McKenzie growled, taking a step forward.

Frank held up one arm to back him off. "And the Leap?" he asked Erica. "Did you sabotage that, too?"

"Yeah." The smirk faded, and she looked troubled. "It wasn't supposed to hurt anyone, though. The ride wasn't even open yet—I figured one of the cars would get smashed up on the last test run, and it would freak everybody out."

That actually made sense, sort of. "But what about the bomb on Cody's skateboard?" I asked. "And the tank? Someone could've gotten killed with those."

"Not likely," she said. "I mean, yeah, that little bomb might've stung a bit if someone was on the board when it went off. But killed? Nah. And how slow and stupid would someone have to be not to outrun a freakin' tank?"

I didn't bother to point out that Sprat had almost gone splat thanks to that tank stunt. Because there was still one big disaster that definitely *had* gotten someone killed.

Before I could mention that, Frank asked about a few of the other dangling loose ends. Like our late-night whitewater chase. Turns out that was Erica. She'd also hacked into her father's cell phone account and sent those texts to Ox about the tractor, and replied to our e-mail to Nick. And she was the figure Lenni had spotted sneaking around that night—the same one who'd dropped the flag on us.

"Never heard of anyone getting killed by having a flag land on them," she said defiantly.

"Get real," I blurted out, too impatient to wait any longer. "If you really didn't want anyone killed, why'd you mess with Bomber Pilot?"

Her jaw dropped. "What?" she blurted out. "No way! I didn't do that! I told you, I wasn't trying to hurt anyone. . . ."

That seemed like kind of a tough argument to make, considering the circumstances. But she stuck to it.

"Whatever," I said as Ox and McKenzie finally dragged her away. "She's just covering—she knows that's the one charge that's way more serious than the rest."

"I guess." Frank watched her go. "I just can't stand the thought that there's a loose thread—again."

"I hear you. But we'll have to let the cops sort it out. Loose thread or not, I'd say this mission is over—finally."

● ● ●

A few days later we were back in Bayport, lounging in our favorite private spot beside the public pool. It was the first chance we'd had to discuss the case without Mom or Aunt Trudy lurking around. It was also my first chance to harass Frank about how Erica's "crush" on him had really just been her keeping an eye on us.

"Whatever. Anyway, I'm glad that one last loose end was finally tied up," Frank commented lazily as he stretched out on his lounge chair.

Yeah, he was changing the subject. I decided to let him—for now, at least.

"I know," I said, feeling troubled by what HQ had told us about that. As it turned out, Erica really hadn't been responsible for that particular disaster. It had been simple human error, probably due to the rush to open the ride. "I can't believe Tyrone managed to sweep that all under the rug. There hasn't been a peep about it on any of the entertainment shows. Or the national news, either. Just a couple of local stories."

Frank turned his head to meet my eye. "Guess it's a good thing for Tyrone it was just some random employee who died and not Sprat or one of the other guests," he said grimly. "Anyway, supposedly Bomber Pilot is back open and one of the most popular rides at GX."

I shuddered. It didn't seem right. But what could we do? We'd already told ATAC—and the police—everything we knew about the incident.

"I wonder how many people Tyrone had to pay off this time," I said. "You know—local cops, inspectors, witnesses . . ."

Frank bit his lip, looking as disturbed as I felt. "I know," he said. "I heard he paid off the dead guy's family, too."

I sighed. "Oh well. I guess it was just an accident—I mean, it wasn't like Tyrone *wanted* anything like that to happen. He's really not a bad guy in most ways."

"Yeah," Frank agreed. "I mean, he did help Ox out of a jam when he needed it. And Erica's over eighteen now—he could've just let her get tossed in jail instead of shelling out for that expensive mental treatment place they're sending her."

I nodded slowly. All the rationalization in the world wasn't going to make what had happened seem right. But what could we do? It was out of our hands.

"Anyway, it must be nice to have that much cash." I glanced around at our decidedly nonluxurious surroundings. "You know—enough to make just about any problem go away."

"Maybe. Then again, maybe not." Frank shrugged.

"Erica had pretty much everything she could want, and she still wasn't happy. Come to think of it, Nick's not exactly a happy guy either."

He had a point. But suddenly I wasn't in the mood to think about it anymore. Rich or not, I was pretty content to be exactly where I was—with another tough mission under my belt and nothing else to worry about on a hot summer day.

"Come on," I said, jumping to my feet. "Last one in the pool's a rotten egg!"

Get ready to meet the next great kid detective,
Steve Brixton!

Here's an excerpt from *The* **BRIXTON BROTHER**^{S}
Book #1: The Case of the Case of
Mistaken Identity

STEVE BRIXTON, A.K.A. STEVE, was reading on his too-small bed. He was having trouble getting comfortable, and for a few good reasons. His feet were hanging off the edge. Bedsprings were poking his ribs. His sheets were full of cinnamon-graham-cracker crumbs. But the main reason Steve was uncomfortable was that he was lying on an old copy of the *Guinness Book of World Records*, which was 959 pages long, and which he had hidden under his mattress.

If for some reason you were looking under Steve's mattress and found the *Guinness Book of World Records*, you'd probably think it was just an ordinary book. That was the point. Open it up and you'd see that Steve had cut an identical rectangle out from the middle of every one of its pages. Then he had pasted the pages together. It had taken over two weeks to finish, and Steve had developed an allergic reaction to the paste, but it was worth it. When Steve was done, the book had a secret compartment. It wasn't just a book anymore. It was a top secret book-box. And inside that top secret book-box was Steve's top secret notebook. And that top secret notebook was where Steve recorded all sorts of notes and observations, including, on page one, a list of the Fifty-Nine Greatest Books of All Time.

First on his list was a shiny red book called *The Bailey Brothers' Detective Handbook*, written by MacArthur Bart. The handbook was packed with the Real Crime-Solving Tips and Tricks employed by Shawn and Kevin Bailey, a.k.a. America's Favorite Teenage Supersleuths, a.k.a. the Bailey Brothers, in their never-ending fight against goons and baddies and criminals and crime. The Bailey Brothers, of course, were the heroes of the best detective stories of all time, the Bailey Brothers Mysteries. And their handbook told you everything they knew: what to look for at a crime scene (shoe prints, tire marks, and fingerprints), the ways to crack a safe (rip jobs, punch jobs, and old man jobs), and where to hide a top secret notebook (in a top secret book-box). Basically, *The Bailey Brothers' Detective Handbook* told you how to do all the stuff that the Bailey Brothers were completely ace at.

The Bailey Brothers, of course, were the sons of world-famous detective Harris Bailey. They helped their dad solve his toughest cases, and they had all sorts of dangerous adventures, and these adventures were the subject of the fifty-eight shiny red volumes that made up the Bailey Brothers Mysteries, also written by MacArthur Bart. Numbers two through fifty-nine on Steve Brixton's list of the Fifty-Nine Greatest Books of All Time were taken up by the Bailey Brothers Mysteries.

Steve had already read all the Bailey Brothers books. Most of them he had read twice. A few he'd read three times. His favorite Bailey Brothers mystery was whichever one he was reading at the time. That meant that right now, as Steve lay on his lumpy bed, his favorite book was Bailey Brothers #13: *The Mystery of the Hidden Secret*. Steve was finishing up chapter seventeen, which at the moment was his favorite chapter, and which ended like this:

"Jumping jackals!" dark-haired Shawn exclaimed, pointing to the back wall of the dusty old parlor. "Look, Kevin! That bookcase looks newer than the rest!"

"General George Washington!" his blond older brother cried out. "I think you're right!" Kevin rubbed his chin and thought. "Hold on just a minute, Shawn. This mansion has been abandoned for years. Nobody lives here. So who would have built a new bookshelf?"

Shawn and Kevin grinned at each other. "The robbers!" they shouted in unison.

"Say, I'll bet this bookshelf covers a secret passageway that leads to their hideout," Shawn surmised.

"Which is where we'll find the suitcase full of stolen loot!" Kevin cried.

The two sleuths crossed over to the wall and stood in front of the suspicious bookcase. Shawn thought quietly for a few seconds.

"I know! Let's try to push the bookcase over," Shawn suggested.

"Hey, it can't be any harder than Coach Biltmore's tackling practice," joked athletic Kevin, who lettered in football and many other varsity sports.

"One, two, three, heave!" shouted Shawn. The boys threw their weight into the bookshelf, lifting with their legs to avoid back injuries. There was a loud crash as the bookshelf detached from the wall and toppled over. The dust cleared and revealed a long, dark hallway!

"I knew it!" whooped Shawn. "Let's go!"

"Not so fast, kids," said a strange voice. "You won't be recoverin' the loot that easy."

Shawn and Kevin whirled around to see a shifty-eyed man limping toward them, his scarred face visible in the moonlight through the window.

The man was holding a knife!

That was where the chapter ended, and when Carol Brixton, a.k.a. Steve's mom, called him downstairs to dinner.

FRANKLIN W. DIXON

THE HARDY BOYS

Undercover Brothers®

INVESTIGATE THESE TWO ADVENTUROUS MYSTERY TRILOGIES WITH AGENTS FRANK AND JOE HARDY!

#25 Double Trouble

#26 Double Down

#28 Galaxy X

#29 X-plosion

#27 Double Deception

#30 The X-Factor

From Aladdin
Published by Simon & Schuster

Nancy Drew ® Simon & Schuster

ALL-NEW FULL-COLOR NANCY DREW GRAPHIC NOVELS!

Coming Soon...

NANCY DREW Graphic Novel #17 "Night of the Living Chatchke" Available May 2009
Nancy Drew travels to Turkey where she uncovers a lost underground city in this all-new adventure!
5x71/2, 96 pages, full-color
Paperback —
$7.95/$8.95 Canada
ISBN-13 978-1-59707-143-7
Hardcover — $12.95/$14.50 Canada
ISBN-13 978-1-59707-144-4

NANCY DREW BOXED SETS AVAILABLE...
Graphic Novels #1-4 Boxed Set
$29.95/$32.95 Canada
ISBN-13 978-1-59707-038-6
Graphic Novels #5-8 Boxed Set
$29.95/$32.95 Canada
ISBN-13 978-1-59707-074-4

Available NOW at your favorite booksellers or order from:

PAPERCUTZ™

40 Exchange Place, Ste. 1308, New York, N.Y. 10005, 1-800-886-1223
MC, VISA, Amex accepted, add $4 P&H for 1st item, $1 each additional item.

THE HARDY BOYS

THE PERFECT CRIME

Play Frank and Joe in an all-new VIDEO GAME!

Available April 2009.

www.hardyboysgames.com

PC CD-ROM SOFTWARE

RATING PENDING
RP
CONTENT RATED BY
ESRB

Visit www.esrb.org
for updated rating
information.

© 2009 Simon & Schuster, Inc. THE HARDY BOYS is a trademark of Simon & Schuster, Inc. and is used under license. Copyright in The Hardy Boys books and characters is owned by Simon & Schuster, Inc. All rights reserved. Reprinted by permission of Simon & Schuster, Inc. All other brands, product names and logos are trademarks or registered trademarks of their respective owners. All rights reserved.